Not Another Bloody Zo

By

Michael Burnsi

Chapter 1

"Wake up, Benny."

"Piss off, Pete."

Benny rolled over and tried to ignore his eager friend.

"I knew you should have gone easy on the beer," said Pete as
he grabbed the end of Benny's sleeping bag and yanked him
out of it.

"Leave it out, Pete! Let me sleep for God's sake," yelled Benny
as he once again rolled over and tried to get back to sleep.

Pete threw the sleeping bag out of the tent and sat down beside
Benny's head.

"Benny?" he said softly.

No answer.

"Benny?"

No answer.

Benny?"

No answer.

"Benny?"

"What!?"

"Oh, you're awake?"

Benny sat up in frustration. Pete was right, he probably should
have gone a little easier on the beer last night. It wasn't as if
there was anyone at the camp area apart from him and Pete to
enjoy it with. His older brother Jason and his friends Arnold,
Stacy and Beth were due to arrive sometime that day to help set
things up for the large, end of school party that weekend.

Benny always looked up to his brother, the good looking athletic popular one who was everything Benny wished he was. It wasn't that Benny had an ugly face, or was overweight or was stupid or even unpopular. He was just very average in everything thing he was and did, and because of that, he went unnoticed. Pete on the other hand, who was the boy who would have got picked last at school at virtually every activity, and was pretty much a social outcast, was at least memorable and known.

Jason always had time for his younger brother and even his slightly weird friend, and had been the one who invited them up for the weekend party. Benny wanted to arrive the day before to get himself settled in with his new surroundings, in the vain hope he would be more comfortable mixing with his brother's older friends.

"What time is it?" he asked Pete, realising he wasn't going to get any more sleep.

"Don't know, but you know that building over by the lake? The one with the big wall around it and all abandoned and run down?"

"Oh yeah," he replied wiping his eyes. "You're serious about scaling the wall and having a look around? We're not kids anymore, Pete. Don't you want to hang out with normal people and do normal stuff?"

"There's lots of time for that later. I'm talking about now. Right now!"

"What are you talking about, Pete?" said Benny as he picked up his T-shirt and put it on.

"It's not abandoned. I saw two army trucks driving out of there at ninety miles an hour. How the hell you did you not hear them?"

"Because I was asleep. Remember?"

"Yeah but you're awake now. So what you think? You want to check it out?"

"I think we need to get some breakfast. I'm starving."

About a hundred yards from where they had pitched their tent, Jason pulled up to the main campsite in his father's four by four. It had been a long drive up which was made longer by the company of his friend, Arnold who had spent the two hour journey, singing along to every song on his play list and boasting about his sexual encounters of the last month, which may or may not have been entirely truthful.

Jason was just glad to finally get out of the car, stretch his legs and perhaps get a break from his friend, even if it was only for two minutes to go for a piss.

"So when's the rest of the crew all coming up?" asked Arnold.

"Benny and Pete should be up already. They finished last week and wanted to get settled in," replied Jason as he opened up the boot of the car.

"Forget them losers, I'm talking about the ladieeees!" sang Arnold, as he danced over to Jason.

"Stacey and Beth should be here today sometime and the rest of them should be up tomorrow," said Jason, covering up how annoying he was finding his friend at that moment.

"Excellent! So I got a day's head start to work on Stacey."

Jason chuckled at Arnold's macho bravado, not really knowing if it was wishful thinking or genuine delirium.

"How will she resist your charm?" he said as he lifted his bag out of the back. "Besides, what about Beth? She's a nice girl too."

"Yeah, guess she is. She'll do if Stacey ends up with you."

"I'm sure Beth will love to hear she's your runner up," said Jason as he handed Arnold's bag to him.

"Naw, I've heard some good stories about Stacey from a few of the guys. Close your eyes and put your hands out. I've got a neat trick."

Jason closed his eyes and held his hands out, almost too trusting. He felt something placed on his wrists and then heard a clicking noise. He opened his eyes to see a pair of pink fluffy handcuffs had been slapped on him.

"What the hell?"

"Yeah, I have it on good authority that Stacey digs that kinky shit. I reckon I'll be banging her before the rest get here," said Arnold as he turned around to check his bag. "I'll let you and Beth have a go with them when we're finished. You know, I reckon Beth could be a really good fu-awkk!"

Arnold shot up straight as he felt the chains of the handcuffs around the front of his neck. Jason held it tight as he stood close behind him.

"I hope you remembered to bring the keys with you, or you'll not be doing any scoring tonight."

"Okay, okay, okay, Jason! Take it easy! I got the keys here," babbled Arnold as he frantically pulled the key out of his pocket.

Jason laughed. "Don't think Stacey would think much if she saw you like this."

"Yeah," Arnold said sheepishly as he unlocked the cuffs. "Hey, Jason. What's that digging into my back? It's hurting."

"Um, just my phone. Yeah. Sorry, man."

Like Jason, Beth wasn't enjoying the long journey to the campsite either and for pretty much the same reasons, namely the friend in the passenger seat. The difference being that while Arnold's chatter was directed towards Jason, Stacey did ninety-five percent of her talking into her phone. The other five percent was spent mumbling and gasping at the constant flow of text messages that occupied her full attention. Eventually the signal to her phone stopped and she spent the remainder of the journey complaining about it.

Despite her lack of consideration for her friend at that time, they were good friends although Beth couldn't help but be envious of Stacey. She was the pretty blonde, all made-up and glowing that caught the attention of the men. Not that Beth wasn't an attractive girl herself. It was just that she didn't feel comfortable plastering herself up like Stacey did. She felt she had a lot more to offer a partner other than just having a nice looking face, which was just what she was told all the time. Her parents, her friends, her cousins, her gay male friends, her friends' boyfriends. Everyone bar the ones who she really wanted to say it, single men who didn't have drool over their feet while their eyes were glued to Stacey.

She decided not to dwell on it and let it bother her, and let whatever is meant to be just take its natural course. Easier said than done, and the more she repeated it in her head, the more it sounded like pretentious bullshit.

"You'll make a great Mrs Right for someone someday soon," Stacey drunkenly mumbled to her at a house party the previous Friday. "But why don't you try being like me and be a Mrs Right Now?"

Three seconds after giving Beth these wise words of wisdom, she puked the contents of the night's drinking over the curtains of the home of the girl whose parents were away living it up in the South of France. Still didn't prevent her from hooking up with four different guys later on, one of whom she spent a considerable part of the evening in the bedroom of the home owners. Obviously they didn't notice or care that Stacy's mouth tasted of a mix of vodka, tequila, her dinner that night and stomach acid.

Beth that night had to make do with a kiss much later in the night from the older brother of the girl throwing the party. He was a reasonably good looking and fairly polite man, who didn't get too stroppy when Beth made it clear that although she did allow him limited liberties with his wandering hands, she wasn't going to be spending the night in his room. It wasn't that she believed in abstinence, but she knew that drunken one off sex with a guy whose name she barely knew wasn't going to work for her.

"Hey, losers! What have you two been up to in that tent all alone?" shouted Arnold, as he saw Benny and Pete walk towards them.

"Don't start," said Jason.

"Doing what you do at the gay bars," shouted Pete cheerfully.

"You cheeky little bastard," laughed Arnold. Suddenly he pushed his face up against Pete's and glared at him. "How many women have you had in your life? I've had five this year alone, including a married woman. What you think about that?"

Pete stood back and looked over to Benny. Arnold smirked at Jason, who was about to reprimand his friend when Pete opened his mouth.

"A married woman? I thought your parents got divorced."

Jason grabbed Arnold before he had time to react. He knew if he had delayed a second more then Arnold would have charged at Pete.

"Let it go, right now," he ordered his friend.

Arnold struggled but Jason tightened his grip.

"C'mon Pete," said Benny, who took hold of his friend, although not as tight as the one his brother had on his friend.

"There's Beth now. Let's say hello."

"Stacey with her? Yeah, let's say hello," Pete replied.

The two younger boys walked towards Beth's car while Jason

and Arnold watched them.

"I don't want any of your crap here," said Jason firmly.

"He started it!"

"I'm serious, Arnold. I don't want to hear any of it."

"Yeah, okay. You can let go of me now."

"Sorry," said Jason as he released his friend. "Now, let's see what state this cabin is in."

"Now we're talking," shouted an upbeat Arnold. "The loooove shack! Let's get it ready for the ladies!"

Beth was glad to get out of the car. She looked around and saw Jason and Arnold unlock the cabin and disappear inside.

"Here let me get your bags there," shouted Pete as he ran over towards Stacey's side of the car. Beth laughed at Pete's not so subtle attempts to woo her friend.

"Hey, Beth," said Benny.

"Oh, hi, Benny. Long time no see. You been up here long?"

"Me and Pete came up yesterday. Spent all day trying to get the tent up. Only the select chosen ones like you and Stacey get to sleep in the cabin this weekend."

"If Stacey hadn't demanded that we get one of the cabin bedrooms then I wouldn't be up here at all. I just hope Arnold doesn't think he can share with me when her and your brother inevitably get together."

"Er, well, you know if you want, you could always crash in our tent."

"Thanks for the offer, Benny" she smiled. "But I'd think I'd get in the car and just go home."

"And don't forget Beth's bag too," Stacey shouted.

They turned around to see Pete loaded up with several bags struggling to walk behind Stacey as she made her way to join the other boys at the cabin.

"It's okay, Pete," laughed Beth. "Sure Benny here will get mine."

"Not a problem," he called back, still carrying the mountain of bags.

She turned to Benny and gave him a poke in the ribs. "You men, eh? You'd all do anything for a pretty blonde, wouldn't you?"

"Where's your bag?" he asked.

"I'm joking, Benny. It can stay in the car until I need it."

"Oh, right," said Benny, feeling a little deflated.

"Once again, appreciate the offer," she said with another smile. "If you want to help, I'm dying for a bite to eat. You got anything here other than beer?"

"I know Jason was bringing the food up for the barbecue tomorrow but I don't know if he brought anything to eat before then. Me and Pete kinda didn't take that into consideration."

"Typical men. No forward planning. Although perhaps I'm not much better."

"We were just about to hit the shop down the road and pick something up, but I guess Pete's busy being Stacey's bellboy."

"Let's leave them to it. I've been driving for near two hours and I fancy a bit of a walk."

"Sounds like a plan." said Benny as he and Beth began to walk down the lane.

"Here, what happened to your car?" he said as he noticed the passenger side was smeared with mud.

"Oh that? There were these two army trucks racing each other that passed us not that long ago. Nearly wiped us out so I guess I'm lucky it was just a huge shitty mud stain."

"Wait a minute! So Pete wasn't making it up? About the army trucks?"

"Believe me, Benny. They definitely weren't made up."

Benny and Beth walked along the muddy track, onto the main road. Benny told Beth how he and Pete had both been learning the guitar for the past couple of months and had a few songs drafted. They even had come up with a few potential names for the band. It was a toss up between Benny's 'Car Crash for My Lover' and Pete's 'Child Grinder Bastards' although they still needed a drummer, bass player and probably a singer. They argued over the merits of having a keyboard player but decided against mainly because they were going to have enough trouble finding three other people willing to hang around with them.

"If I could sing, or could play an instrument, I'd join your band," joked Beth, "But let me know when your first gig is, and I'll be there."

"Thanks, you'll probably be the only person in the audience."

"Maybe not, you could ask this guy to come along. Think he looks like a rocker?"

Ahead of them on the other side of the road, a young man in a leather jacket, torn jeans and shades stumbled along towards them.

"Looks like he had a good night last night, maybe I should have hung out with him instead of Pete," whispered Benny.

"Maybe he wants to join your band, he's coming over."

The man had noticed them on the opposite side and adjusted his path so he would meet them when he crossed the road.

"God," muttered Beth. "What drunken crap is this guy going to come out with?"

"H-hey, man!" called Benny, when the man was only a few steps away. "How's it going?"

The man never answered but simply raised his hands and lunged towards Benny. Before Benny had an idea what was going on, the man had his hands tightly wrapped around his throat.

"Hey!" screamed Beth, as she forced her way between them, and with all her might, gave the man a massive shove in the chest. The man stumbled backwards and then tripped hard onto the ground.

"You okay?" she asked Benny. All he could do was nod his head, the shock of the random unprovoked attack left him speechless. Beth turned around to see the man slowly getting up to his feet. She slowly walked backwards, making sure Benny was still behind her as she kept her eye on the man.

"What's your problem, dickhead!? Huh!?" she screamed.

He looked straight up at her and groaned. His sunglasses had slipped off in the fall and his eyes were exposed. Beth and Benny both gasped. His eyes were like two red orbs. No whites or coloured iris or even a black pupil. Just completely blood red eyes.

And he was still coming closer.

Chapter 2

"So which room are me and Beth getting then?"

"Ah, you two fine ladies will be staying next door to us in the Mahogany suit," said Arnold as he opened the door to the bedroom. Inside was a wardrobe and a bunk bed in the corner.

"Do you prefer being on top?" asked Pete, still carrying Stacy's bags.

"What?" exclaimed Stacey.

"Top or bottom. Which one you sleeping in?" replied Pete innocently.

"Oh right, bottom. There's no way I'm attempting to go on top." She said, looking at the set of beds.

Behind her back Arnold rhythmically moved his pelvis in and out while making slapping motions with his hand.

"What are you doing, Arnold?" asked Pete in a fake naiveté, causing Stacey to spin around and Arnold to straighten up a micro second too late.

Stacey's face never gave anything away as she looked at the two boys and gave a slight smirk. She walked out of the bedroom and into the one next door where Jason was unpacking his bag.

"I'm going to kill you, you little shit," whispered Arnold, as he walked over towards Pete.

Pete immediately dropped the bags he was carrying, sprinted past Arnold and out the door. Arnold paused for a brief second before giving chase, shouting threats about what he was going to do to Pete when he caught him.

Jason heard the commotion from the next room.

"For Christ's sake, will you two knock it off!" he shouted. He turned around to see Stacey standing in the doorway.

"Oh, hi, Stacey. I see you and Beth made it up ok. You like the room?"

"I think I like yours better," she said, as she slowly walked towards Jason and closed the door behind her.

"Um, well they're pretty much the same," said Jason. "But if you and Beth want to swap then I'm sure Arnold won't mind." Stacey smiled and put her arms around Jason's neck.

"I think some sort of swap can be arranged, don't you think?" she said as she moved her mouth closer to Jason's. He quickly pulled away.

"What?" shouted Stacy in disbelief. She always got what, or rather who she wanted, and wasn't used to this type of rejection at all.

"Sorry, sorry," he muttered as he turned around and dug around in his bag.

"No, seriously, Jason. What's your problem? You enjoyed it last time?"

"Last time?" thought Jason. "Oh, that time. What were we? Thirteen?"

"It's Beth, isn't it? You'd rather be with her? Is that it? It's okay. I understand. I mean, I know compared to her I'm just seen as a dumb blonde who..." rambled Stacey.

"No, I don't want to be with Beth. She's a nice girl and all…."

"You've someone else? Who is she? Do I know her? She coming up here?"

"No there's no one else. It's just…"

"It's just what? You haven't decided to become gay have you?"

Jason said nothing.

"Oh," said Stacy.

"That doesn't look normal, Beth," said Benny, who had managed to find his voice.

"No shit," she said.

They both continued walking backwards, constantly keeping their gaze on the man with the blood red eyes. Benny held Beth by the arm as he helped guide her as they walked. He felt it was the least he could do to try to act remotely masculine in front of her.

The man kept staggering slowly towards them with both his arms held out, saying nothing bar a few low groans.

"You think we should just run for it back to the camp?" Benny suggested.

But before Beth could answer, they heard the sound of a car traveling at high speed from behind them.

"Oh shit," shouted Benny, as he realised the car was out of control and heading towards them. He quickly snapped out of his shocked state when it reached several meters away, forcing him to push Beth and himself out of the car's path and onto the ground. Missing them both the car then carried on until it smashed into the red eyed man, knocking him back onto the road and then driving over him. The car then stopped, leaving the flattened body twitching on the ground.

"Holy shit!" exclaimed Benny looking up.

"Get off, you're hurting me," shouted Beth, who Benny was still lying across.

"Sorry, sorry," said Benny as he quickly stood up and put his hand out to help Beth.

"It's okay, thanks by the way," said Beth taking his hand, realising that she just snapped a little at the guy who saved her.

"Is that guy dead?"

"Don't think so, probably just fatally injured."

The car door opened and a man wearing a priest's dog collar and a blood-stained black suit staggered out.

"Jesus Christ, you kids alright?" he called out. He walked towards them, obviously in a lot of pain as he winced with every step. When he reached the still twitching body of the red eyed man, he raised his foot above his head and brought it crashing down.

Beth and Benny stared opened mouthed, as the alleged priest continued to stamp on the man's skull until it caved into a mess of bone, flesh and blood.

It was Beth who managed to regain her speech first.

"What are you doing?! Are you crazy or something?!"

"Me?" said the priest as he wiped the blood off his boot on the body of the undoubtedly dead man.

"Yes, you!" Beth shouted back. "Who do you think I'm talking too?"

"Sorry if I drove a little close to you…"

"A little close!?" interrupted Beth. "You nearly killed us!"

"Sorry," said the priest looking down at the ground, holding out his blood stained hands. "My companion he…."

The priest took a breath and wiped his face with his hand, not realising he now had blood on his face. He tried to speak again.

"My companion turned while I was driving, and I was a little distracted." he said as he pulled out a silver hip flask from his pocket and took a long swig from it. "I didn't know that was one of them until I hit him. I'm just glad I didn't kill a normal person."

He downed the contents of the flask and then threw it behind him. He then dropped down to the ground, held his head in his hands and began sobbing.

"You think he's okay?" Benny asked Beth.

"You can't hide up there forever," Arnold shouted up at Pete, who had somehow managed to climb up to a sturdy tree branch fifteen feet from the ground. Secretly Arnold was slightly impressed that he was able to move and climb at such quick speed and ease.

"Why don't you come up and get me then," jeered Pete, half hoping that Arnold would give up and leave him alone.

Arnold thought for a moment. He didn't like how Pete was almost goading him to climb the tree, but he didn't fancy going up to get him. He knew that if he did manage to get on the same branch, Pete would probably panic and fall. And even though he did try to ruin his chances with Stacey, Pete dying or at the very least being severely injured, would probably put an end to the party all together.

"You know something? You can stay up there for all I care. You can watch while I get a bit of action. What you think of that?"

"Doing it with yourself doesn't count," Pete shouted back.

Arnold gritted his teeth. "It's always the same with you, isn't it? The same shitty jokes, the same stupid shit. You ever get sick of it? Ever get sick of being a loser that nobody likes? I thought Benny was bad, but at least he'll probably get laid before he's fifty."

Pete said nothing but fumed silently on his branch. Arnold just shook his head and stormed off, leaving Pete alone with his thoughts.

He stared off into the distance, wondering how long to give it before climbing down. The view he got from up there was amazing and he could see for quite a distance. As he stood up and squinted, he thought he could see a large group of people slowly walking towards the camp. They were just too far away for him to make out but he assumed they were the rest of the people coming up for the party that weekend. Although he could have sworn Benny had told him they weren't due until tomorrow, and it did strike him odd that they were all walking rather than traveling in their cars.

"Looks like it's kicking off early," he said to himself.

Chapter 3

Benny peered into the car while Beth stood beside the priest with her hand on his shoulder. On the passenger side he could see there was a man's blood soaked body slumped against the door. When he looked closer he could see that the man's throat had been torn out. Benny immediately recoiled in horror and looked over towards Beth and then he stared at the priest's hands. He now knew why they were so bloody.

"I think we should maybe report this to someone," he called to Beth.

"You won't have to," sobbed the priest. "They all know. Everyone knows now and if they don't, they will soon."

"What do you mean?" said Beth, trying to hide the waver in her voice.

The priest took a deep breath. "We have a couples retreat up the road. A place where we can help people who were having trouble in their relationships. It's such a nice little place. Or it used to be."

"What happened?" asked Beth.

The priest took another deep breath.

"We were sitting down for breakfast, all seven of us. I just went out to check on my papers, when I heard screaming. I ran inside and saw that Martin, Barbara and Alan were...."

"Were what?" asked Benny, feeling uncomfortable.

The priest looked up at Benny, his eyes flowing with tears.

Beth knelt down beside the priest.

"Please," she pleaded. "What happened?"

"Their eyes! They were red! Red eyes!"

"You mean like that man that you just run…" said Benny.

"Quiet, Benny," said Beth. "Let him finish. Go on, sir."

"Robert had run, the cowardly little bastard," snapped the priest. "He left his wife and Elaine behind to get…"

He stopped again to release another sob.

Benny and Beth both looked at each other and then down to the priest. They were both about to ask the priest to once again continue when he shouted.

"They were tearing them apart! With their bare hands! They tore those two poor women apart and ate them!"

"What?" said Benny and Beth in unison.

"I froze," said the priest softly. "God forgive me, I froze. I can still hear the screams of those two poor women as their friends butchered them. And all I could do was stand there."

"Did you say they ate them?" asked Benny.

"What happened then? Where are they now?" said Beth.

"Barbara came at me," continued the priest shaking. "Martin and Alan continued to eat but she looked right at me and came straight for me. She had her mouth open and I could see blood and flesh inside it. Elaine and Janet's blood and flesh. Then she tried to take a bite out of me but I pushed her to the ground and got out of there. I ran outside and to my car to find that miserable bastard sack of shit Robert hiding inside. I probably still would have ended up ripping his throat out even if he hadn't turned."

"You killed him?" said Beth, taking a step back from the priest. She motioned with her head for Benny to do the same also.

"No! He turned! He was dead once he became one of those red eye bastards! It was him or me!"

"I really think we should call the police," said Benny.

"I told you, son. It will do you no good. We drove along the road and there were others. Not just the three of us. I must have counted thirty of those red eyed devils along these roads since this started. They were all the same, their mouths stuffed with blood and meat. We saw one poor woman, screaming for her life as half a dozen of them fiends pinned her down and tore her apart like a pack of wolves. God save that poor woman's soul. It was too late to do anything for her. If only we found her sooner. We could have picked her up in time! We might have been able to save her!"

"Why has this happened to them?" said Beth, trying hard to stop her voice trembling.

"Cannibals!" shouted the Priest, standing up and taking a firm grip of both of Benny's shoulders. "That's what they are! Soulless, inhuman, insane cannibals! There's no emotion in those blood eyes! They kill, and gorge and then eat!"

"Okay, okay. We get it," said Benny trying to break free from the priest's grip. "So what should be do then?"

The priest stared at him with an even greater look of panic on his face.

"Nothing! There's nothing we can do! It's the end. We're being punished! Repent! Repent!"

"Jesus Christ!" shouted Benny as he finally broke free from the priest's grip.

"Jesus save us! Jesus save us!" screamed the priest over and over again. Then he stopped and stared directly at Benny.

His eyes had turned red.

Chapter 4

"So how long have you been…you know?" said Stacey.

"Pretty much forever I guess," said Jason.

"Really? But didn't you and Ursula Brown..."

"Yeah we did."

"And what about Lindsey McCann?"

"Well, after her I knew for sure."

Stacey sat down on the bed, a little shocked. Jason sat down beside her and handed her a can of beer.

"If it helps, you're the first person I've told," he said as he opened one himself.

"Er, thanks," said Stacey, still feeling a little unsure. "Um sorry, I kind of pushed you though. I didn't mean it when I asked if you were."

Jason laughed. "Don't worry about it. No harm done. As long as we're still friends." He leaned over and gave her a small kiss on the top of her head.

"Thanks," she said, smiling nervously back.

"You okay?"

"Yeah, I'm fine. So, um, if it's okay and you don't mind me asking, what's your type of guy then?"

Pete carefully slid down the tree to the ground below after he was sure Arnold had completely stormed off. He began to mutter to himself. As much as he didn't want to let on, guys like Arnold really annoyed him. He never could understand why they were the ones who got the girls. He also couldn't understand why he even bothered coming up when he knew the party would be full of people like Arnold.

He slowly strolled back towards the main camp, hoping that maybe Arnold had cooled off and had no interest in pounding him into the ground.

Arnold thought about going back to the cabin, but then figured that Jason and Stacey were getting busy with each other and thought best to leave him. He pulled out the fluffy handcuffs from his pocket and sighed at them. He then placed them back in his pocket.

"Don't give up, Arn, don't give up, Arn" he muttered to himself. "There's still Jenny and Angela, you can get one of them. Maybe both. At the same time." A big smile came across of his face.

"You're right. Thanks, Arn. You're the best." he said to himself again. He then noticed Pete wandering aimlessly into the main camp.

"There's a few guys already here," said Pete pointing to some people walking along the road to their camp.

"Can't be. It's not until tomorrow the party starts." said Arnold as he walked over to get a better view of the road.

"You want me to tell them to go away then?"

"Don't be stupid," said Arnold as he shoved Pete out of the way. "Who is it?"

Pete glared back at Arnold for pushing him. "How am I supposed to know? They're your friends."

"There's three of them. Don't recognize any of them."

The three figures slowly continued to walk towards the camp while Arnold and Pete watched them.

"They're not any of our lot, that's for sure" said Arnold when he could make out that the figures were three middle aged men.

"You better go tell them to piss off."

"Me? Why do I have to..." said Pete, who turned around to see Arnold had walked away.

"Dick," he muttered to himself.

"Okay, okay," said Stacey, trying to keep a straight face. "How about this one. What about Tommy? Would you?"

"Your older brother? I don't know, he looks alright."

Stacey laughed. "Is that a yes then?"

"You know, for someone who I though was going to blow up when I turned her advances down, you seem to be finding this all quite funny."

"Aw, you know I'm only messing. I've never had a gay best friend before."

"Oh, so you're going to be my fag hag then?"

The front door to the cabin opened.

"That must be Arnold," said Jason. "Listen, Stacey..."

"It's okay, Jason," said Stacey as she rubbed the inside of Jason's leg. "Your secret is safe with me."

"Thanks," he said. "That you, Arnold?"

"Yeah," came Arnold's voice from the other side of the door.

"Erm, I'm just going to grab a beer and I'll leave you two

alone."

"Don't be running off now," said Stacey as she hopped up to open the door. "Come on in, we're not doing anything." She gave Arnold a cheeky wink. Arnold looked over to Jason, who just shrugged his shoulders, obviously knowing more than he was letting on.

"Um, yeah," said Arnold nervously as he walked in.

Jason got up and handed him a beer.

"Tell me you haven't killed Pete then," he said.

"No, he's perfectly fine," said Arnold.

"Help! Help me!" came a scream from outside. It was Pete.

"Oh Christ! What should we do now?" said Benny walking backwards once again making sure Beth was behind him.

"Just stay away from him," replied Beth, holding on to Benny, trying to ensure there was enough distance between them and the priest.

"You think we could get lucky a second time and somebody could else could run him over? Maybe a bishop this time, or the Pope himself?"

The priest had turned his head and noticed the two of them backing away from him. He gargled some inhumane noise and began to stumble towards them with his arms stretched out.

"Think we've used up our luck," said Beth. "We can out run this guy no problem. Think you can run back to camp?"

"Run?"

"Yes, Run."

"But won't that lead him back there? Is that wise?"

"Benny, we're walking backwards and he's not going to catch us. I hardly think he's going to be able keep up."

"Yeah, okay," said Benny, as he and Beth both turned around to face the direction they were moving in.

"Oh, shit!" they both said in unison.

Just less than sixty yards up the road, five people were stumbling towards them. All five with blood eyes.

They turned back towards the priest who was only a few footsteps away and was getting closer.

"Go round him!" shouted Beth, as she gave Benny a shove which pushed him to the left of the priest while she ran past him on the right.

"Get in the car!" she shouted once they had left the priest behind snarling in confusion. Beth jumped into the driver seat and started the engine right away.

"Benny, get in now!"

She turned to see that Benny was staring at the corpse sitting in the passenger seat.

"Um, Beth. There's somebody in the seat. I'll just get in the back!"

"Like hell you will! I'm not driving with that thing there!" she shouted back. She leaned over and pushed the corpse out. It hit the ground with a sickening thud, leaving a bloody mess beneath it.

"Now get in for Christ's sake!"

Benny stepped over the corpse and into the car, closing the car door just as the priest's hand reached out to grab him. The priest released a terrifying howl as Benny glanced around to see that he had trapped his hand in the door.

"Oh God, sorry," stammered Benny.

Beth drove off at full speed. As the priest was dragged along the road chunks of his flesh were shredded off like cheese to a grater.

"Is he still hanging on?" asked Beth.

"Not by choice," said Benny opening the door, releasing the priest. "That's him gone now!"

Beth looked in the rear mirror and saw the priest bump and roll along the road out of sight. She then hit the brakes, performed a three point turn and started heading back.

"You going to finish him off?" asked Benny.

"No! What do you think I am?" she replied. "We got to get back to the camp and get the others. I hope we're not too late."

"I'm sure they'll be fine," said Benny. "We handled them two easy enough, didn't we? Jason and Arnold should be able to handle it."

Chapter 5

"Pete! What's wrong?" said Jason as he dashed out of the cabin with Stacey and Arnold following behind. All three of them stopped dead when they saw Pete holding up his right forearm. Blood was following from a large gash.

"He bit me! The bastard bit me!" he hysterically shouted.

"Who?" shouted Jason.

He didn't need to wait for an answer. He saw the three men strutting towards them, with the one closest to them drooling blood from his mouth. He then noticed the man's eyes. Blood red.

"Stacey, get the first aid kit in the cabin. Get this arm bandaged," he shouted, as he directed Pete over towards Stacey.

Jason wondered if there was any point trying reasoning with the man who had bit Pete. He thought not and threw a punch to the man's jaw knocking him back a step. Jason stared as the man simply turned his head towards him and opened his mouth, baring his blood stained teeth. Before he realised it, Jason had fired a second punch to the man, this time successfully knocking him to the ground.

"What's with those eyes?" shouted Arnold, who was having difficulty taking everything in.

"It's not just him, look at these two!"

Two other red eyed men were slowly coming closer. Jason

gave a kick to the head of the one that he had knocked down, before taking a defensive stance against another one.

"I got this one, you get the other," he yelled at Arnold.

"What!?" replied Arnold, who was not prepared when the one closest to him reached forward and grabbed him by the shoulders. Arnold lost his balance and fell onto his back with the red eye falling on top of him.

"Jesus, this bastard's trying to bite me," shouted Arnold, holding the red eye by the throat as it gnashed its jaws at him.

"Hang on!" said Jason, as he shoulder charged the remaining red eye who was vertical. He managed to knock him over which freed him up to help Arnold. He ran over to his friend, taking a firm hold of his attacker by the throat and then threw him off.

"Thanks," said Arnold as Jason helped his friend up. "What up with these freaks?"

"I don't know, Arn. Where's Pete and Stacey?"

"They're in the cabin. What do we do now?"

Jason was lost for an answer. All three of their attackers had recovered and were bringing themselves to their feet. Arnold looked around on the ground and picked up an empty beer bottle. He looked at Jason for approval before throwing it straight into the face of the one who had attacked him. The bottle shattered, leaving a glass shard in the red eyes face, but despite this, it didn't slow him down. He, along with the other two, kept moving towards them.

"Aw, shit," muttered Arnold. "What you reckon, Jason? Get to the cabin? Find a weapon there?"

"Okay! Go!"

Together the two of them ran into the cabin and slammed the door shut. Inside Stacey was wrapping Pete's arm with an entire bandage roll while he sat watching her intensely. Arnold did notice that Pete's eyes were not so subtly staring at her chest, but didn't feel it was the time to say anything. Instead he grabbed the chair that Pete was sitting on, yanked it from under him and then wedged it under the door handle.

"Hey!" shouted Peter as he lay on the floor. "I was sitting on that."

"Sorry, man," said Arnold dismissively as he joined Jason at the window, who was watching the three red eyes stroll towards the cabin.

Stacey helped Pete up and continued to wrap his arm. Pete continued his gaze at her chest.

"What's going on out there?" she asked, clearly distressed.

"I don't know," said Jason, still watching them from the window. "That one's getting too close."

"That just isn't normal. Did you see their eyes?" said Arnold

"Yeah, hard to miss. You got anything that can be used?"

Arnold looked around and a fire extinguisher caught his eye. He grabbed it and showed it to Jason.

"That might help," said Jason, as he took it off Arnold. "Get the door. One of them is right at it."

"What you planning?" asked Arnold.

"Just open the door when I say, and then get ready to close it again!"

Arnold pulled the chair away, nodded at Jason and swung the door open. Standing in the doorway was the red eye who had Pete's blood around his mouth. Before it had time to react to the sight of its four potential victims, Jason swung the extinguisher over his own head and down onto the red eyes skull. The blood flowed from the red eye's head as he fell down hard. Jason raised the extinguisher up and brought it crashing down on the red eye's face, causing it to cave in.

"Jason! Did you just kill that man?" shrieked Stacey.

Jason never answered but threw the extinguisher at one of the others before running back into the cabin. Arnold slammed the door and placed the chair back against the door handle.

"To be fair, that man did take a chunk out of me," said Pete holding up his bandaged arm.

"He had to do it," said Arnold. "Those guys want to kill us. It's us or them. Right, Jason?"

Jason meekly nodded. The realization of what he had done was beginning to sink in. He wondered if maybe he went too far.

"Hey guys, you think I could have a bit more bandages?" Pete called out, holding his arm out They all looked to see the blood continued to soak through his dressing.

"Here, this should help," said Arnold, holding a roll of duct tape.

"Er, is that safe enough?" Pete asked.

"If you don't stop moaning I'll use it to tape your mouth shut," snapped Arnold as he quickly wrapped the tape around Pete's bandaged arm. "There. That should stop you bleeding all over the place."

"Thanks," said Pete, half annoyed but also half grateful. "So what's the plan then? We stay here or we get out?"

Stacey and Arnold looked over to Jason for a suggestion. It took him a moment to notice that they were looking at him for an answer.

"We need to find Benny and Beth."

"Oh God," said Stacey. "I hope they didn't run into them."

"I'm sure they're fine. Benny wouldn't let anything happen to Beth." said Jason.

"Yeah, she'll be safe with Benny," piped up Pete. "Did you know he completed the first Resident Evil in two hours twenty minutes?"

"Did you also know I wasn't joking about taping your mouth shut?" said Arnold.

Before Pete could respond with a witty come back, two pairs of fists began banging the door from the outside.

"That must be the other two," said Jason, looking out the window again. "Crap! This isn't good."

"What is it?" said Arnold joining him at the window. "Sure we could take the two of them?"

"Not them," said Jason. "Them over there!"

About dozen people, had entered the main camp area from the road. They were men and woman, of different ages, sizes and shapes but they all had two things in common. They all had blood red eyes and they were all walking towards the cabin.

Chapter 6

Beth drove the car back to the camp as quickly but as safely as possible.

"Hang on," she said, while making a hard turn onto the road to the campsite.

They both gasped in horror when they saw a large number of red eyes had surrounded the cabin.

"We're too late!" said Benny.

"No, they might still be alive," shouted Beth as she drove straight towards the cabin. She slammed the brakes on and then blasted the horn. Immediately all the red eyes stopped and turned their attention towards the car.

"Look, there's Jason!" shouted Benny, catching sight of his brother looking out the window. "They're still alive!"

"Let's try and keep it that way," said Beth, as she put the car in reverse and sped backwards.

"Who is that?" asked Stacey.

"It's Benny and Beth!" said Jason. "They're distracting those things! We can make it to my car and get out of here."

"That's too dangerous!" said a frightened Stacey.

"I know but we've no choice," said Jason, preparing to open the door. "We need to run as fast as we can and avoid them things."

"Don't worry, I've got you," said Arnold as he gently took Stacey by the arm. "Just stay with me."

"What about me then, Romeo?" said Pete. "I'm a casualty

here."

"It's your arm that's injured, you prick," replied Arnold.

"There's nothing wrong with your legs. Yet."

"Seriously, will you two ever shut up?" said Jason, as he slowly opened the door and peered out.

"Alright! We've got their attention!" cheered Benny.

"Hopefully we've got it long enough for them to get out," said Beth.

Beth continued to hold the horn down as the red eyes migrated towards the noisy stationary car.

"That's it!" shouted Benny. "We've done it! Now quick, drive over to the side here! They should be able to get to my dad's car now!"

Beth put the car into first gear and pressed down on the accelerator. The back wheels spun but unfortunately for them, they were stuck in a huge puddle of muddy water that Beth hadn't realised she had stopped in.

"Aw shit!" exclaimed Beth, as she frantically switched the gear to reverse and tried again. Still the car was stuck. "This isn't good. I'm going to need a push."

"You're joking, right?"

Beth looked up and saw Benny's fears weren't unfounded. Instead of surrounding the cabin, the red eyes had now started to swarm around the car.

"Now! Run!" shouted Jason to his friends, as he held the door open. "Get to the car!"

Arnold held onto Stacey as he led the way. Pete followed straight after them while Jason stayed at the back to make sure the three of them got to the car.

He only took several steps out of the cabin when he saw that Benny and Beth were trapped, surrounded by red eyes.

"No, please no." Jason said to himself as he could see a look of panic on both their faces, as the glass of the car began to crack. He glanced quickly to see that the other three were clear of immediate danger, then ran to the group of red eyes.

"Come get me instead! Come get me, you bastards!" he shouted. A few of them noticed him but still the majority of them continued to beat on the car. Out of anger and frustration he grabbed one of red eyes from behind and threw it to the ground as hard as he could. He grabbed a second one and did the same. Now all of the others had his full attention.

"That's it, you dumb bastards! Come get me!" he shouted as he slowly drew them off the car. As he walked backwards he waved to Beth and Benny to get out of the car. Beth slowly opened her door and carefully slid out, with Benny following her.

"Get to Dad's car," shouted Jason. "I'll double back and meet you…Arghhhhh!"

Jason had spent too much time keeping track of the red eyes coming towards him, that he forgot completely about the two that he had thrown to the ground. He looked down to see the first one had its teeth sunk into his calf muscle.

"Jason!" screamed Benny, moving towards his brother.

"No, Benny! Get away! Get away now!"

The second red eye had risen behind Jason and took a huge bite out of the back of his neck. The other dozen or so red eyes saw the kill being made and swooped in themselves. Beth put her arms around Benny both in an attempt to shield him from the sight of his brother being killed and to stop him from running in.

"I'm sorry, Benny. I'm so sorry," she said, trying to hold back her own tears.

Jason felt several hungry jaws clamp down on his body, and excruciating pain as they bit huge chunks of flesh from him. With the last bit of life still left in him, he pulled out a set of keys from his pocket, and raised his hand high above the rabid swarm.

"Benny!" he screamed one last time, as with his last remaining strength threw the keys high up in the air. They landed by Beth's feet and she quickly picked them up.

"We got to go, Benny. I'm sorry, but we have to go!" she literally cried, holding him by the arm and dragging him towards the car. All Benny could do was to stare in disbelief as the body of his brother disappeared under a mound of the savage red eyes. His brother's cries of pain had stopped but the sound of limbs being pulled out of their sockets and then broken sounded ten times worse.

Arnold raced towards Benny and Beth.

"Jesus Christ! Those bastards...."

"Arn, we need to go," pleaded Beth, still trying to pull Benny away. "It's too late for Jason."

Beth handed Arnold the keys and then turned to face Benny.

"Jason did this so we could get away. We have to go now."

"Yeah, I know," stammered Benny.

"Well let's go now," shouted Arnold taking a firmer grip of Benny and dragging him back to the car with Beth following behind. Pete and Stacey waited at the car for them, both looking deeply concerned.

"Jason? He didn't..." blurted out Stacy.

"He didn't make it," said Arnold unlocking the car and getting in the driver seat. Pete took the shotgun seat while Benny, Beth and Stacey jumped in the back.

"Where we going?" asked Pete.

Arnold never answered. He started the engine and drove as fast as he could out of the camp. He didn't know where he was driving to, but he intended to get as far away as possible.

"I couldn't do anything," said Benny softly to Beth. "Jason's dead and there was nothing I could do."

Beth put her arm round Benny and pushed his head to her shoulder.

"There was nothing any of us could have done. There was far too many of them and you would have been killed too. Jason's sacrifice would have for nothing."

Pete turned around to face them.

"Those things might move slow, but they can move faster than you think when they're hungry."

Arnold punched him hard in the arm.

"Ow! What was that for? Oh, right. Yeah sorry, Benny."

"It's okay, Pete. Don't worry about it," sighed Benny.

"The asshole is right though," said Arnold. "They're a lot more dangerous than they first look. If we see any more of them we're going to have to be careful."

They passed several lone red eyes as they drove along the road. Arnold resisted the urge to mow them down as he saw each one, but thought best not to risk damaging his late friend's father's car and to just keep moving.

"I'm not getting any signal," said Stacey checking her phone. "Anyone got anything."

"I left mine in my car," said Beth.

"Mine died last night," said Benny.

"I got nothing," said Pete. "What about you, Arnold? Not that you should be looking at your phone while you're driving."

Arnold reached into his pocket and was about to pass his phone over to the girls in the back, when he realised he was holding out the fluffy handcuffs instead.

"Shit," he muttered, as he quickly stuffed them back into his pocket. Fortunately for Arnold, the girls in the back never noticed.

Unfortunately for Arnold, Pete did.

"That one of those new fancy phones, Arnold?" he asked, with a hint of innocence. Arnold never answered.

They approached a small newsagent shop which looked very lonely on the forest road. Arnold stopped the car outside it.

"Why are we stopping?" a frightened Stacy asked. "We should keep going."

"There's bound to be a land line or something inside," he said. "Wait here."

"Be careful, Arnold," said Beth, as Arnold got out of the car.

"I'll go with him," said Benny getting out of the car also.

"You sure you should, Benny?" asked Beth.

"Yeah, I'll be fine. Be safer than Arn going in there alone. Just stay in the car and keep the doors locked."

"Okay. You be careful too, Benny," said Beth, giving a nervous smile. Benny smiled back

"We'll be as quick as we can," he said closing the door. He ran over to join Arnold at the shop door.

"Just stay behind me," ordered Arnold. "If there's anything here, I'll deal with it. You just watch my back, okay?"

"Yeah, no problem," he said. "Just do a better job here than you did at the camp."

Without responding, Arnold opened the door and walked into the shop.

Chapter 7

"Hello! Anyone here?" shouted Arnold.

Although the shop seemed deserted, many of the shelves had been knocked over with various tins, cereal boxes and broken bottles spread out over the floor.

"Nobody about. Wonder who trashed the place then?" said Benny inspecting the mess.

"There must be a phone somewhere here," said Arnold as he picked up a broom.

"Try through that door behind the counter," replied Benny. "What you doing with that broom? You going to clean up here?"

"Just being safe," he said as he marched towards the counter and jumped over it. "Stay here, I'll be back in a minute." He then disappeared through the door.

"Dickhead," muttered Benny under his breath. He thought about going back to the car when he heard a huge clatter from behind the door Arnold had gone through.

Benny spun round to see Arnold falling backwards through the door with an obese balding man with blood red eyes falling on top of him. He raced over to the counter and looked over to see Arnold flat on his back, desperately holding off the large man who was attempting to take a huge bite out of his throat.

"Jesus, Benny! Help me!" cried Arnold, sounding not as bravado as he had done so a few moments earlier.

Benny, like Arnold before, jumped over the counter and landed behind the red eyed man. He looked around for something to use a weapon when he spied the broom Arnold had been carrying lying in the doorway. Quickly he snatched it up and from behind held the broom tight around the front of the red eyes neck. With all his might he pulled as hard as he could, giving Arnold enough time to wiggle out from underneath the red eye.

"Keep holding him!" shouted Arnold as he got to his feet.

"Hurry!" shouted Benny, who was completely unprepared for how strong the man was. "I can't hold him!"

Arnold quickly glanced around before deciding on the cash register. He grabbed it off the counter, breaking off the cables that connected it and then smashing it into the face of the red eye.

The force nearly knocked Benny out himself, who was flung several feet back before falling over. The red eye, however, was still standing, despite its face being left a bloody mess. It looked up at Arnold, and as it groaned at him, a mouthful of teeth fell out.

Arnold raised the register again and rammed it against the red eye much harder. Benny was barely able to get out of the way as the red eye fell back against the wall. Its skull turned to a flatted mess as Arnold continued to grind the register against the wall with the red eye's head in between.

He took a few steps back, dropped the register to the ground and examined the damage he had done. Any resemblance to a head was now gone, as it had now become a huge pulp stain on the wall behind. The red eye's body slid down, leaving a bloody trail on the wall as it fell to the floor.

"Thanks," said Benny as Arnold put his hand out to help him up.

"Yeah, you too." replied Arnold, giving a subtle pat on Benny's arm.

"Anything in there," said Benny.

"Didn't get a chance to check. Fat boy here jumped me."

Benny picked up the broom and handed it to Arnold.

"Here you go. Maybe it's clear now?"

"Okay, let's try that again. You got my back, Benny?"

Benny nodded and they both walked through to the large store room at the back. The first thing that caught the eye of both of them was the blood drenched remains of a mangled body in the middle of the floor.

"Guess we know what fat boy had for lunch," said Arnold dryly.

"I can't even tell if that was a man or a woman," said Benny.

"Well, I'm not going close enough to find out," replied Arnold, picking up a long brown coat off a rack and handing it to Benny. "Here, cover that up."

Benny threw the coat over the body has best as he could without getting to close the gruesome sight.

"There got to be a phone somewhere," muttered Arnold.

"People still use land lines, right?"

"Wait!" whispered Benny. "You hear that?"

"Hear what!"

"Listen! I hear someone. Over there!" said Benny pointing to another door hidden at the back.

"So what do you mean he just changed," asked Pete.

"He changed into one of them," said Beth. "He was fine and then his eyes turned red like those things out there, and then he tried to attack me and Benny."

"So why did he change?" said Stacey. "Was he sick or something? Like he caught a disease or something?"

"I know as much as you do," said Beth. "I've no idea what made him or those other people turn the way they did."

"So how do we avoid it then?" said Stacey. "I mean, there's nothing to say you or me or even Pete turning. He was bit by one of those things!"

"Woah! Woah!" said Pete, a little flustered. "I feel fine. Arms a little sore still but I'm okay. Honest!"

"Calm down, Pete!" said Beth. "And, Stacey, you calm down as well! And stop asking me stupid questions when you know I don't know the answers."

Stacey tutted and turned to look out the window so she wasn't looking at Beth. She wasn't used to being reprimanded and she didn't like it at all. Beth instantly felt bad that she had upset her friend but she knew she didn't say anything that wasn't true. She was just as scared as Stacey was. It's just she was hiding it a lot better. She thought about saying something to Stacey to make her feel a bit better but thought it was best to leave Stacey to get over her huff in her own time. It worked in the past.

"How is your arm, Pete," asked Beth.

"It's fine, honest," he said, holding it out for Beth to see. Despite being bandaged with duct tape, blood was still dripping through.

"Okay I believe you," she said, moving her head away from it.

"We should still get that looked at as soon as we can. Once Benny and Arnold are back we'll head on to a hospital and then…well. I don't know really. Head back home and hope the police or whoever sorts it out soon."

"So I guess the party's over then?" said Pete. "And there was me looking forward to getting shot down over and over again by all the pretty girls."

"You're welcome to go back to the camp if you want, Pete," said Beth. "Me and Stacey will wait here for the guys to come back and you can go hang out with those things in the woods."

"You think it's just the woods it's happened?" said Stacey, still looking out the window. "I mean, could this all be happening back home?"

"I hope not," said Beth.

"You open the door, get out of the way and I'll smash its head in," said Arnold, trying to sound confident.

"Just a second," said Benny moving his ear closer to the door.

"I think I hear crying."

"What? Just open it and get out of the way!"

"No, Arnold," said Benny. "It's a kid."

Benny flung open the door to the small store room to see a small girl with long blonde hair, no more than six or seven years old, wearing a purple dress. She looked up at Benny with tear stained eyes.

"Hey, there," said Benny, crouching down to the girl's level and putting his hand out. "It's okay, what's your name?"

"Kerry," she sniffed.

Benny moved slowly towards her.

"Kerry? That's a nice name. Do you know where your parents are?"

Kerry looked down and slowly shook her head.

"Don't worry, we'll find then for you," said Benny. "Arnold, go get Beth."

Arnold quickly left the store room leaving Benny still holding Kerry's hand.

"I'm Benny and me and my friends are going to make sure you're safe and with your parents soon."

Kerry, still looking down, squeezed Benny's hand tight.

"Hey, it's going to be alright, Kerry," said Benny gently squeezing her hand back. "I tell you what. You like chocolate? I bet you do. Am I right?"

Kerry shrugged her shoulders, still not looking up.

"Oh, I bet you do. How about we fill our pockets with some chocolate bars here and have a little feast? Wouldn't that be fun?"

Kerry nodded her head.

"Yeah I knew you would like that," laughed Benny. "I love chocolate too. I'm surprised I haven't turned into a chocolate bar with all the bars I eat."

"Hey, what's your name?"

Benny turned around to see Beth standing at the doorway with Arnold behind her.

"This is Kerry," said Benny. "She's a little shy but me and her are going to eat all the chocolate bars here. Isn't that right, Kerry?"

"Don't you look in pretty in that dress?" said Beth as she knelt down beside her. "Who was looking after you?"

"Grandad," said Kerry sadly. "He told me to hide here."

"We're going to help find him for you," said Beth picking Kerry up in her arms. "Do you live in the town down the road?"

Kerry nodded as she put her arms around Beth.

"Well that's where we'll go. You live there with your mummy and daddy?"

"Yes. And my brother."

"We better get you home then. I want you to close your eyes really tight for me, Kerry, and just think of your house and your mummy and daddy and brother. Keep them closed until we get outside. Can you do that for me?"

"Yes," said Kerry, hugging onto Beth and closing her eyes.

Beth motioned to Benny and Arnold to follow her out.

"I'll just pick up a few things and see you out there," Benny said to Arnold.

"Don't take too long," said Arnold. "We need to stay on the move." He then followed Beth and Kerry out of the store.

Benny picked up an empty cardboard box and quickly loaded it with cans of soft drinks, chocolate bars and crisps. He walked out of the store room and just on the counter beside where the till used to be, he spied a phone.

"How'd you miss that, Arn?" he said to himself as he placed the box down onto the counter. He picked up the phone but before he had a chance to dial a number, he heard noises on the other end. At first, it sounded like a low irregular static buzz but then he could hear a voice as well. He put his hand over his other ear and concentrated on the sound from the phone.

"Hello?"

Suddenly the voice became clear. It wasn't a singular voice but several different ones, all whispering at the same time.

"*Waaan*"

"What?"

"*Theee*"

"Who is this?"

"*Zerro Kay Zerro*"

"What does that mean?"

"*Aree*"

"Hello? Hello? Can you hear me?"

"*Waaan Theee Zerro Kay Zerro Aree!*"

Benny held the phone out as the collection of voices repeated the chant over and over.

"*Waaan Theee Zerro Kay Zerro Aree!*"

"Waaan Theee Zerro Kay Zerro Aree!"

"Waaan Theee Zerro Kay Zerro Aree!"

"Waaan Theee Zerro Kay Zerro Aree!"

He slammed the phone down and took a deep breath wondering what on earth just happened. He scooped up the box full of treats and then ran out of the shop to the car outside.

Chapter 8

"I like your hair," said Kerry.

"Kerry likes your hair, Stacey," said Beth. "It's the same colour as hers."

"Um? Thanks," said Stacey, unsure what to make of Kerry sitting on Beth's lap watching her.

"I think yours is nicer," whispered Beth into Kerry's ear, making the little girl laugh.

"I still like hers," laughed Kerry.

Stacey looked over to Kerry and gave a smile although her eyes showing her mind was still elsewhere.

Benny leaned forward in his seat so he was closer to Pete.

"Something's not right," he said.

"Really?" said Pete, sarcastically. "There was me thinking this is normal for this neck of the woods."

"No, I mean really not right. I think this is something much bigger than we think."

"What you on about, Benny?" said Arnold leaning across to get closer to the conversation the best he could while still driving.

Benny looked over towards the girls sitting beside him and figured he wouldn't be able to tell Arnold and Pete about what he heard on the telephone without them hearing bits of it.

"I'll tell you when we get to town," he said, leaning back into his seat.

Beth looked over to Benny and gave a concerned look making sure Kerry was unable to see.

"It's fine, don't worry," he said, lying blatantly.

After several minutes driving, with Beth and Kerry laughing and joking, and the rest sitting in silence watching and listening to them, they arrived on the outskirts of a small town.

"This is where you live, Kerry, isn't it?" said Beth.

"Um, I'm not sure. My daddy knows," said Kerry, starting to get upset.

"It's okay, don't worry," said Beth, pulling Kerry closer to her. "We'll get you home. I promise."

"It's not a big place but there's bound to be a police station," said Arnold. "We can take her there and let them know what's going on back there."

"Maybe they know already," said Pete. "There were quite a few people wandering about there. That kind of thing should be hard to miss."

"Well we haven't seen any police or anyone else, have we?" said Stacey. "Surely there should be someone in authority or something telling us where to go, right?"

"Look, Arnold," said Beth. "Just drive into town and we'll play it from there. There's bound to be someone who can help."

Arnold did as Beth suggested and drove into the town along the main street that ran through it. Although the buildings and shops appeared to be open, there was initially no sign of life. Suddenly Arnold slammed the brakes on hard, causing everyone to be thrown slightly forward.

"Shit, Arnold," shouted Pete.

"Language, Pete!" scolded Beth.

"Yeah, watch your language," said Kerry, waving her finger at Pete.

"Um, sorry. So, er, why'd you stop?"

"Because of them," said Arnold pointing up ahead.

A group of three people were huddled over what seemed to be a bloody lump on the ground, from which they were frantically pulling pieces of it and stuffing it in their mouths. It wasn't until one of the three eater turned around with a human arm in its hands that they became fully aware what the bloody lump was.

"Close your eyes again, Kerry," said Beth, trying hard to stay calm. "Think of that happy place for me. Can you do that for me?"

"Okay, Beth. I'll do it."

"If I were driving," Pete said quietly to Arnold, "I would consider putting this thing into reverse, and driving at high speed in the other direction. Just a suggestion."

"Yeah..." said Arnold, still staring at the feeding frenzy up ahead. He tried changing to reverse but in his nervousness, he ended up grinding the gears, making a loud racket and still failing to reverse the car.

"Shit!" he shouted, as he continued to try. "Sorry, I mean, sugar!"

"Sometime today would suit us fine," said Pete.

"Do you want to get out and walk?" snapped back Arnold

"At this rate, I might be better doing that," replied Pete.

The commotion had got the attention of the three up ahead who had stopped eating and were looking towards the car. All three of them unsurprisingly had blood red eyes.

"You need push the button under the gear stick," shouted Benny from the back.

"Got it!" said Arnold, finally getting it in reverse. He put the accelerator to the floor and the car sped backwards. One and a half seconds later there was a sickening thud from the back of the car causing Arnold to instinctively slam the brakes on. He turned around to see a large blood stain on the back window.

"What did we hit?" yelled Stacey. "Did we hit someone?"

BAM!

They all jumped as a bloody hand appeared from below and slapped the windscreen. A thin, ragged man then pulled himself up and stared through the back windscreen with his blood red eyes.

"Where the hell did he come from?" shouted Benny.

"Same place as them," said Pete, looking towards the front. They all looked outside to see a group of about fifty red eyes making their way out of the side streets and towards the car.

"It's not looking much better over here either," said Benny pointing to his side of the car. Another group, much bigger than the first was approaching from the side. Both groups were ten second away from swamping the car.

Arnold once again, put his foot down hard on the accelerator and reversed the car, flattening the lone red eye that had been banging on the windscreen to an even greater mess.

"Dammit!" shouted Arnold, hitting the brakes again. "There's more of them!"

A third group of nearly thirty had now appeared from behind them effectively surrounding them on three sides.

"Can't you just ram them?" shouted Pete.

"It's not a bloody tank, you dickhead," snapped back Arnold. "There's too many of them!"

"Just get us out of here, Arnold," yelled Beth, holding tight onto Kerry who had her head buried deep into her shoulder.

"I'm not stupid!" Arnold shouted back. He put the car into first gear and drove it down the side street which didn't have red eyes flowing from it.

At first driving along the street, even at high speed was going well for them. There were a few red eyes dotted along it but no large groups like there were behind them. However, when they reached the end of the street they were greeted with the sight of several cars, crashed and mangled together. Effectively blocking the road.

"Aw, no!" said Arnold, braking the car unexpectedly again. "Not good, not good at all!"

"We can't go back," said Benny, looking through the bloody back windscreen. "There must be over a hundred of them."

Everyone except Beth who was making sure Kerry view of the events was covered, looked behind them. Sure as Benny said, at the far end of the street, a large mob of red eyes. Benny's estimation of over a hundred was a little off as by now, due to the amalgamation of the three groups, along with the addition of several smaller clusters, the total was over two hundred. Two hundred red eyes barely a hundred yards away and were getting closer.

"Arnold!" shrieked Stacey, "Get us out of here!"

"We got to go on foot," said Benny, surprising everyone by getting out of the car.

"You're mad," cried Stacey, still looking at the approaching swarm of red eyes.

"We've no choice," shouted back Benny as he helped Beth get out while Kerry still clung on to her. "We got to move now!"

Pete and Arnold both jumped out of the car as well. Arnold quickly opened Stacey's door and took her arm.

"He's right!" said Arnold, gently pulling her out. "Just stay with me!"

"What way?" said Beth.

"Well that way's out," said Pete pointing to the mob. "So I vote this way."

"Just move!" shouted Arnold, who then led the way around the mash of cars, holding onto Stacey. Benny gently pushed both Beth and Pete in the same direction and followed behind.

"You okay? You want me to take her?" Benny said to Beth.

"It's fine, I got her," she wheezed back. Benny could tell she was having difficulty but didn't want to admit it. He put his arm around and helped to pull her along. Whether it was any help or not he wasn't sure but he felt he had to do something. Although the distance between the large group and them was beginning to increase they were still the occasional red eyes along the street. They were far away so they weren't in the path of the six but their presence alone was enough to keep them feeling nervous.

"Arnold, stop!" said Stacey breathless. "I can't go on!"

Arnold stopped and looked at her. He then looked around and noticed the main group of red eyes was far enough away that they could comfortably stop for twenty seconds. Five seconds later Benny and the others caught up.

"We need to hide somewhere safe," said Benny. "What about one of those shops?"

"What if there's some of those things in there?" said Stacey.

"We'll just have to risk it! Go for that one before they see us!" said Arnold picking out a charity shop. He pulled Stacey along while the others followed behind. He reached the door and pushed it open. Quickly he ushered Stacy, then Beth and Kerry, then Pete and finally Benny in before taking a final look outside and running in himself. He slammed the door and noticed the bolt locks at the top and the bottom of the door. He reached up, locked the top then knelt down and locked the bottom.

"That's not going to keep them out," said Pete staring out the front window.

"We'll be fine," said Arnold, pulling him away. "They didn't see us going in and as long as you keep your ugly face hidden, we should be safe."

"You hear that, Kerry?" said Beth putting the little girl down and kneeling beside her. "We're safe."

"Where are we?" she said, opening her eyes and looking around. "It smells funny in here."

"That's just Arnold," said Pete. "You get used to it eventually."

"I will throw you out there, you know," said Arnold.

"Seriously, will you two just stop?" said Beth frustrated. "They might not be able to see us, but they certainly will hear us at this rate."

"Yeah," piped up Kerry. "You two better stop."

"That's right, Kerry," said Beth smiling at her. "Will boys ever learn?"

While the others were arguing Benny had walked to the back of the shop, hoping that there may be something that may provide useful. He had no idea what he could find in a dusty shop filled with racks of second hand clothes, books and ghastly household ornaments. He was about to walk back to the main group at the front, when he heard nervous breathing from behind one of the book shelves in the corner.

Benny leaned over to see a middle aged man in a fancy suit, huddled behind it, shaking uncontrollably. He hadn't noticed Benny who moved around to get a closer look at the man's eyes. They were normal.

"Who are you?" said Benny.

The man looked up startled and quickly stood up.

"No! No! No! No! No!" he shouted, looking over to the group at the front of the shop. He looked over to Benny and then back to the group.

"Hey, man. It's okay. We're not one of them," said Benny.

"No! No! No! No! No!" he repeated, frantically turning his gaze from Benny to the group then back again.

"Are you listening?" said Benny. "We're not going to hurt you." Benny put his hand out but the man shoved Benny hard to the floor, then looked towards the front window of the shop.

"What's your problem?" shouted Arnold, walking over with conviction towards the man. "You starting something?"

"Arnold, wait," said Stacey, taking a grip of Arnold's arm. "He could be one of them."

The man stared directly at Arnold then back the window.

"No! No! No!" he shouted as he ran towards the window.

"What you doing?" shouted Arnold.

The man never answered but jumped through the window, smashing it to pieces and slicing himself in the process.

"You crazy bastard!" said Arnold as he watched the man continue running into the middle of the street, towards the now visible large group of red eyes

"No! No! No!" he repeatedly shouted as he fell down to his knees, making no attempt to escape. In what seemed like no time he was surrounded by the large group red eyes and then he was gone, disappeared under a feeding frenzy from a small portion of the group.

There wasn't anything left of the man for the rest of the group of red eyes but there attention had now been turned towards the broken window were the man had initially ran out of. While several of the red eyes who had got lucky and continued to eat at the unfortunate man the rest of them began to march towards the charity shop.

Chapter 9

"This looks like trouble," said Pete.

"You think they know we're here," said Stacey peering round the broken window. Just as she spoke, the red eyes let out a collective groan and increased their shuffling movement towards the direction of their hiding place.

"Yeah…," said Pete, "I think we're screwed."

Benny turned around and spied a door right at the back of the shop. He turned the handle and found it unlocked.

"Yes!" he exclaimed. "Everyone! Back here now!"

Opening the door revealed a narrow set of winding wooden steps.

"You go up first, Arnold," said Benny. "Make sure it's clear!"

Arnold was slightly taken back with Benny giving him an order but he knew not only was there no time to argue but that it really was best for him to go first. To argue would only make it look like he was scared to go up ahead, and he figured the last thing the group needed was for him to look like a coward.

Benny kept an eye on the window at the front as he waved Beth, Kerry and Stacey on up the stairs.

"That leads up," said Pete, also looking frantically back at the front window. "We need to get out."

"What choice do we have, Pete? None!"

The debate was broken by the sound of crunching glass as several red eyes had reached the window and were entering the shop.

"Point taken," said Pete as he raced up the stairs.

Benny went through and slammed the door shut just as Arnold came running down with a chair and wedging it against the door.

"That's not even going to hold a fart back," said Benny.

"I'm not finished! Get your ass up the stairs!"

Benny followed Arnold up to the room above the shop which appeared to be a small living quarters with a bed, couch and a kitchen area. Beth was sitting on the edge of the bed cradling Kerry while Pete and Stacey were looking out the window overlooking the street.

"Give us a hand, will you, Pete," shouted Arnold lifting one end of the couch. Pete came over and lifted the other end but as he did, he felt the pain from his arm injury forcing him to drop the couch narrowly missing his foot.

"I got it," said Benny quickly taking his place. Together they brought it over to the top of the stair case.

"They're inside," shouted Stacey. "I can hear them."

"They're not getting up here!" said Arnold defiantly. With Benny's help he pushed the couch all the way down the staircase until it was up against the door, smashing to pieces the chair that was there holding the door firm.

"Anything else up there?" said Benny.

"Just a few more crappy chairs," said Arnold, assessing how effective the barrier was going to be. "How about we throw the fridge and cooker down as well?"

The groans from the red eyes on the other side of the door

became more evident and more worrying.

"Better than nothing," said Benny racing back upstairs. Pete slumped down in the corner, holding his injured arm, while Beth and Stacey watched in amazement as Benny and Arnold relentlessly threw wooden chairs, two tables, a bedside cabinet and the fridge down the stairs, adding to the barricade. They both stood at the top of the stairs, breathless but satisfied that they had done enough to keep them safe for a bit longer.

"You couldn't have taken some food out of that fridge first?" said Pete, slowly raising his head.

Arnold looked at Benny, offended with what Pete had just said. He was just about to snap when Beth spoke.

"You alright, Pete? You don't look too good there."

"I'm okay," he said smiling weakly at her. He barely had his eyes open as the sweat poured from his head. "Arm's still bloody killing me though."

He held it up for the others to see that the blood had begun to soak right through the duct tape.

"We need to get you to a hospital," said Beth.

"Yeah, I was thinking that too," said Pete, lowering both his arm and head. "Might have a few problems getting there though."

The thumping on the door down below began and the groans became more audible.

"They know we're here, "said Stacey. "Can they get up here?"

"No," said Arnold.

"Maybe," said Benny.

"Eventually," said Pete.

"We can't stay," said Beth. "We'll have to think of a plan."

"I'm telling you, those stupid bastards will bang on that door and then give up," said Arnold.

"I don't know, Arnold," said Benny. "There are a lot of them. They may just keep at it and they could break through eventually."

"We just need to make sure we're gone by the time they get up here," said Beth. "What other way is there to get out?"

Stacey ran to the back of the room and pulled back a dusty worn curtain. The back window overlooked an alleyway that ran behind the shop.

"I can't see any of them down here," said Stacey as she looked in all directions along the alleyway. "You think we can get down there?"

"That's about ten feet down, give or take," said Arnold joining her at the window. "Shouldn't be too difficult."

"Does that window open?" said Beth.

"Stand back," said Arnold, ripping the curtain of the rail and wrapping it around his hand.

"Be careful, Arn," said Stacey, as Arnold turned his head away from the window and smashed his fist against the glass, breaking most of it away. He then knocked along the edges of the frame to remove the remaining glass.

Benny stuck his head out the window and looked down.

"You think we can get out this way?" he asked.

Arnold pulled him back and stuck his own head out. He looked straight down, then left and finally to the right.

"Right, it's all clear down there," he said as he pulled himself back inside. "I don't see any point hanging here any longer here, unless you want to catch a rest or something."

"Seriously, Arnold?" said Stacey, "How can we sleep when those things knowing we're up here? Just get us out of here!"

"Beth?" asked Benny.

"Stacey's right," sighed Beth, still holding tight onto Kerry. "We got to get somewhere safer."

"I agree too," said Pete, dragging himself to his feet. "Preferably somewhere where I can get a burger."

"Okay, well lets get a plan sorted," said Benny. "What's the best way to get everyone out?"

Arnold never answered but climbed out the window and lowered himself so he was hanging from the window sill.

"Careful, Arn," said Benny, as he watched Arnold let go and drop to the ground. He landed on his feet, stumbled over but quickly regained his composure.

"Who's next?" said Benny looking at the rest of the room.

Everyone looked at each other, not knowing if they could make the drop the same way Arnold did.

"I'll go next," said Pete, gabbing the bed sheet from the bed. "We can hold this out to catch the rest of you."

"Not a bad idea, Pete," said Benny as he patted him on the back.

"Catch," he shouted to Arnold as he threw down the bed sheet.

As the bed sheet fell it opened up and caught Arnold like a fish in a net.

"You stupid bastard," shouted Arnold as he pulled the sheet off himself. Just as he got free he looked up to see Pete had jumped off the ledge and was hurtling towards him. Before he knew it, Pete had landed on him and they were both lying flat out on the ground.

"Argh, my arm! My arm!" shouted Pete as he jumped up clutching his wound.

"What the hell were you thinking?" yelled Arnold, slowly getting up. "You trying to kill us both?"

"Will you two shut up?" called Beth from above. "Those things aren't deaf!"

"Yeah, sorry," said Arnold. He took a few deep breaths and noticed Pete was huddled over, still clutching his arm. "Hey, Pete. You okay, man?"

"Yeah, I'm fine," sniffled Pete. "Here, take an end of this sheet. We got to get the rest out."

Arnold took one end of the sheet while Pete did his best to hold the other end tight.

"You're next Kerry," said Benny.

"Don't be scared," said Beth gently as Kerry began to fret. "Just close your eyes and I promise it will be over before you know it."

"I want to go with you," cried Kerry as she held tight onto Beth. "Please don't leave me."

"I won't. I swear, Kerry."

"You'll have to jump together," said Benny. "You think you can manage that?"

Beth nodded and while still holding Kerry tightly, kicked a wooden box towards the window. She stood on the box to get herself and Kerry high enough to step through the window and onto the sill outside. She gently turned herself around with her back out, closed her eyes and gave Kerry a small kiss on the top of her head.

"Just close your eyes tight, Kerry. We'll be down before you know it."

Beth leaned back and let herself fall down. Both her and Kerry opened their mouths to scream but before they could they reached the bed sheet.

It was Pete who screamed. He made sure he held the sheet tight until Beth and Kerry had landed safely, but once they did he dropped it and fell to the ground letting out a quick painful scream.

"Kerry!" shouted Beth. "You okay?"

"Y-Yes," said a shaken Kerry, hugging Beth tight.

"Pete? You alright?" she said, noticing Pete lying on the ground with his back to them.

"C'mon, Pete," said Arnold, walking over to him. "We still got Stacey and Benny to get out."

"Yeah, just give me a sec," he said, slowly getting back to his feet.

"Are you ready?" asked Arnold, giving him a pat on his good arm.

Pete got up and once again took a hold of the sheet the best he could. Beth set Kerry down and held part of the sheet beside Pete.

"Just wait there, Kerry," she said. "Ready when you are guys."

"You go first," said Benny. "You need a hand?"

"Yeah, thanks," said Stacey nervously as she took Benny's hand and climbed out onto the outside window sill. She looked down and froze.

"I can't do this," she said under her breath.

"Sure you can," said Benny, patting her gently on the side of the leg. "Tell you what, I'll lower you down and then let you drop. You wouldn't have as far to fall."

Before Stacey knew what was going on, Benny had hopped up so he was standing right beside her on the very narrow ledge.

"Now what?" she said, still unsure of what Benny was planning to do.

"Um, just give me a minute to figure this out..." muttered Benny, making it clear to her that he really was unsure of what to do.

"Hurry up, will you!" shouted Pete.

"Not so loud, Pete," scolded Beth.

"Okay, okay," Benny said to Stacey bringing his arms around her from behind and holding her loosely. "If I just put arms, er, around you and then, hold you over the edge..."

As Benny spoke his instructions, he tightened his hold of Stacey and slowly lifted her up. He turned slightly to hold her over the edge, but he misjudged his own strength and he felt himself tumble forward with Stacey in tow.

They both somersaulted together as they fell with Benny ending up below Stacey. As the pair hit the target, it slowed their descent slightly but Benny still touched the ground with Stacey landing on top of him.

"Stacey! Are you okay?" said Arnold as he lifted her up off Benny.

Stacey starred back wide eyed and nodded. She looked up at the window, then down to the ground were Benny was lying with Beth and Pete around him. She covered her mouth and gasped.

"You're bleeding, Ben," said Pete.

"What?" said a shell-shocked Benny

"Your nose. Must have been when Stacey landed on you." Benny put his hand to his nose and then looked at it to see blood.

"I've had worse," said a still shaken Benny, as both Beth and Pete helped him get up to his feet.

"I'm sure you have, Superman," laughed Beth. "Guess you fall for blondes too."

"Wha-? No, no, it's not like that. I just..."

"Hey, Arnold. Seems Benny gotten further than you have." smirked Pete.

"Very funny," snorted Arnold. "Everyone ready to move on? Benny?"

"I'm fine," he said picking up the bed sheet and wiping the blood from his nose. "What's the best way out of here?"

"Is it worthwhile trying to get back to the car?" said Beth scooping Kerry back into her arms.

"Won't they still be blocking the way?" said Stacey, who was beginning to regain her composure.

"Maybe," said Arnold. "But then again, they may have all followed us to here and cleared the way. We'll just have to be very careful when moving on. I'll lead, everyone stay behind me. Benny, think you can look after the back?"

Everyone turned to Benny who had just finished wiping the blood from his nose.

"Yeah, no worries," he said throwing the bed sheet down. "Ready when you all are."

With Arnold at the front, the group made its way along the alleyway and round to the side of the main road. Arnold peered round the corner to see the massive crowd of red eyes congregating around the charity shop.

"Shit," he muttered. "Lucky we did leave when we did. Look at them all trying to pile in."

"There's so many," said Beth. "They'll break through that door in no time at all."

"Well it's a good thing we're not still up there then," said Pete.

"Won't they figure out we went out the window?" said Stacey worried.

"Doubt it," said Arnold. "They're pretty stupid. Dangerous but still stupid."

"Well lets not underestimate them," said Beth. "You think we can still get to the car?"

"Yeah, I think so," answered Arnold. He strained to look down the street which ran at right angles to the one they were hiding on. "It looks clear down there. If we make a run for it, it should lead us back to the car."

"What about the ones who blocked the way?" said Stacey, who was beginning to breathe quickly.

"They're all occupied with the shop we were just in," replied Arnold. "There'll be a few stragglers along the way, but I think the bulk of them won't even notice us."

"Well there's a few of them that are going to notice us very soon," said Benny from the back of the group. "Look!"

Benny pointed to the far end of the alleyway. Three red eyes, two male and one elderly female, were slowly walking through as yet unaware of the six of them at the opposite end.

"Whatever we're going to do, I think we should do it now," said Benny. "Arnold, if you can lead us to the car, I'll make sure everyone follows you."

Arnold gave a quick nod to Benny. "Everyone ready? Remember we're faster than them. Just follow me and let me worry about anything in our way."

Stacey put one arm around Beth and held Kerry with the other. She gave them both a nervous smile.

"We can do this, girls," she said.

"I know," said Beth

"Now!" whispered Arnold.

Chapter 10

They ran out of their hiding place and along to the other side of the road keeping as far away from the group of red eyes blindly feeding into the shop as possible. Arnold led the way doing his best to match his speed with his slower moving friends. He looked back as often as he could to see how they were doing. He could see the frightened faces of the three girls and it really hit him that this group was depending on him. Everyone he knew always looked up to Jason, but now, with Jason gone it was up to him to fill his shoes.

Beth held onto Kerry. The only thing that she was focusing on at that moment was keeping that little girl safe. Carrying her while running had made her ache, and she was still upset about losing Jason, but all that was pushed back. She felt she had something more important than herself to focus on.

Stacey kept close as she could to Beth and Kerry. She was glad her friend was with her but at the same time it made her feel fairly useless. Not only was she keeping the three guys in check, she was also looking after a little girl who had taken to her. That was the type of respect and influence she dreamed about it. She could catch the attention of any hormonal teenager or man but in situations like this, she knew nobody would care what she thought or did.

Pete kept right behind the trio of girls. He kept his good arm on the back of Stacey, helping to move her and the other girls along. He knew she probably wouldn't notice or care that he was helping. They were all looking at Arnold. They always did as far as he was concerned. A guy who makes jokes and doesn't take himself too seriously never gets a look in. Especially in life and death situations.

Benny followed behind. The fall still had him winded but he didn't want the others to know. Everyone else had gotten themselves down without any harm including a six year old girl. He wondered why Jason got all the good genes and he ended up the loser, and wished his brother was still here.

Arnold was doing fine keeping things together but Benny felt he still was relying on some of his and even Pete's ideas. If Jason was here he would lead in full confidence and they wouldn't be in this much danger.

Arnold led the progression towards the blockage of cars, where their own was waiting for them. As they had predicted and hoped the huge crowd of red eyes who had initially blocked their route had moved on. A few of them still remained but were not close or quick enough to endanger the group as they darted by.

"That was a lot easier than I thought it was going to be," said Pete.

Arnold opened the back passenger door of the car and helped Beth, Kerry, Stacey and Pete in, before slamming it shut.

"Looks like I was right," he said to Benny who ran over to the front passenger side. "The crowd has cleared."

"Good call, Arn," said Benny, "Now get us the hell out of here."

Arnold reversed the car, turned it and carried down the road that they originally came along. Despite the massive singular group of red eyes having moved on, there were still several of them along the streets. Some of them oblivious to the car passing by, while others turned their heads and attempted to stumbled along after it.

"We need to get out of the town," said Benny. "In fact, I think we should avoid towns altogether. Those things are bad on their own but when they get together like that they're very dangerous."

"So where should we go to?" asked Stacey, leaning forward so she was between Benny and Arnold. She looked at both of them in turn. Neither one of them had an answer. She then leaned back in her seat and sighed.

Arnold continued driving without anyone saying a word. It wasn't long before they were out of the town and on a deserted country road.

"What's on the radio?" asked Pete.

"I don't think this is the time to listen to music," tutted Stacey.

"No, he's right," said Benny, turning the radio on. "There's got to be some news or something."

A surge of static over the speakers caused everyone in the car to wince in pain.

"Jesus! What station's that, Benny?" said Pete. "Sounds like the shit my sister plays."

Benny turned the volume down and began to scan through the

radio stations. Nothing but static on all of them, until Benny heard a voice. A voice he had heard before.

"*Waaan Theee Zerro Kay Zerro Aree!*"

"What the hell is that?" said Arnold, looking down at the stereo.

"*Waaan Theee Zerro Kay Zerro Aree!*"

"Just keep your eyes on the road, Arn," said Beth. "We've enough problems as it is."

"*Waaan Theee Zerro Kay Zerro Aree!*"

"I don't like it," sobbed Kerry.

"Neither do I," said Beth. "Turn it off, Benny."

"That's what I heard on the phone," said Benny as he switched the radio off. "What phone?" asked Arnold.

"Back in the shop. I found one there but that was all that was coming through."

"So what is it? What's it saying?" said Pete.

"Your guess is as good as mine, shrugged Benny. "Doesn't sound good whatever it is."

"My Granny's house is over there," said Kerry pointing out the window.

"Really?" said Beth. "Your Granny lives near you?"

"Yeah. On this road. Up a little bit."

"You want us to take you to see your Granny?" said Beth. "Won't that be fun?"

"Yeah," said Kerry as she held onto Beth tighter.

"It's not this house up here, kid?" said Arnold, pointing to a large white house in the distance.

"That's it." she said.

"Maybe your mummy and daddy are there too," said Beth. "I bet they'll be glad to see you."

Benny and Arnold glanced over to each other. They both could tell that the other was thinking the same thing. The chances of Kerry's parents or anyone else near the town being still alive were virtually non-existent.

"I'll be glad to get to the toilet," said Pete. "I'm dying for a crap here."

"For goodness sake, Pete," exclaimed Beth.

"I nearly went a couple of times earlier on to be fair."

Kerry laughed out loud. "You're funny."

"You think I'm joking?" he replied deadpan, but then gave a Kerry a cheeky smile.

After a few minutes driving the car turned into the drive way of the lone house on the road.

"This definitely the place, Kerry?" said Arnold bringing the car to a stop.

"Yeah."

"Just your Granny lives here?" said Beth.

"Yeah."

"Don't see much sign of life," said Benny, opening the door and stepping out.

"Just be careful, Benny," said Beth. "It might not be..." She stopped mid sentence when she remembered that it was Kerry's grandmother's house and didn't want to upset the little girl any further.

"Don't worry," he said. "I'll just check to see if it's clear and…"

Benny froze when he saw the barrel of a shotgun in his face shoved in his face.

"Shit!" he said, instinctively putting his hands in the air.

"Who are you?" demanded a piercing woman's voice.

Benny looked round the barrel to see the fire arm was held by a short, old lady with a mean looking face.

"M-Me?" he stammered.

"Granny!" shouted Kerry.

"Kerry?"

The old woman turned to see Beth opening the door and bringing out Kerry.

"Kerry!" she said shrieked with joy. Her stony face melted and a smile beamed across her face. She lowered the gun and bent down to embrace Kerry. The little girl hugged her grandmother. "You're alive! You're alive! Thank God! Thank God! Thank God!" Tears of joy rolled down the old woman's face.

Arnold, Stacey and Pete all got out of the car and joined Beth, who was watching the family reunion with a smile. The old woman looked up at Beth.

"Thank you so much for bringing her back to us."

She then stood up, held Kerry's hand while still holding the shotgun in the other and walked over to Benny.

"Sorry about that, young man," she said, wiping her eyes with back of the hand holding the shotgun.

"Yeah, don't worry about it. I've lost track of the amount of times I've nearly died today."

"I'm Maggie. You better all come inside. It's not safe outdoors."

Still holding Kerry's hand, Maggie led them to a side door into the kitchen. She placed the shotgun on the kitchen board, then once everyone had entered the house she closed the door and bolted it.

"Thanks. I'm Beth. This is Benny, Pete, Stacey and Arnold," said Beth pointing to each of her friends.

"Nice to meet you nice young people. Please sit down," said Maggie pointing to the large wooden table. "You too, Kerry."

Kerry ran straight over to Beth and jumped up on her knee.

"Looks like somebody has made a new friend," laughed Maggie, as she put a kettle on. She joined the others at the table still smiling, and looked at their solemn faces. The smile faded from Maggie's face.

"Forgive me. I can tell you've been through a lot. I really appreciate keeping Kerry safe. You're all good people."

"We just did what anyone else would do," said Beth looking at Kerry proudly. "She's a lovely girl."

"She certainly is," said Maggie. She turned to look at Benny. She could tell that his melancholy was deeper than the others. "You've lost someone close, haven't you."

Benny nodded.

"We wouldn't have made it this far if it weren't for Benny's brother," said Arnold, reaching over and giving Benny's shoulder a good shake.

"What happened to your arm, son?" said Maggie finally noticed the bloody duct tape wrapped round Pete's arm.

"This?" said Pete, holding his arm up. "Apparently I got mistaken for a happy meal. I'm not too happy about it."

"You might joke, but I know that must really be hurting you. Let me look at it for you."

"No, no, I'm fine really," said Pete, hiding his arm under the table.

"Don't be such a baby," said Maggie getting up. "Come into the living room with me and I'll look at it. The kettle will be ready if anyone would like a cup of tea."

Despite Pete's protests, Maggie still took a hold of his good arm and coaxed him with her through the door into the hall.

"How about that," smirked Arnold. "Pete's finally scor-" He cut himself off mid sentence when he looked up and saw Kerry sitting on Beth's lap.

"Um, anyone want a cup of tea then?" he asked, as he stood up.

"Now stop being a big baby!" shouted Maggie from the living room.

"I'm telling you, I'm fine!"

"I'm not going to hurt you!"

"This from the woman who had a shotgun pointed at us two minutes ago?"

"Now you're just overreacting. It was your friend I pointed it at."

"Oh, I guess that makes it alright then?"

"Arnold, go and make sure Pete doesn't offend Maggie," sighed Beth.

Arnold left the kitchen, into the hall where he looked into the living room to see Pete trying his best to keep his back to Maggie.

"C'mon, Pete," said Arnold. "Let her help you out."

"I'm fine!" he snapped back, staring straight back at Arnold.

"Whoa! You better calm down right now, Superman," said Arnold, surprised at Pete's outburst.

Benny and Stacey both came into the room from the kitchen.

"You sure you're okay?" said Benny slowly approaching Pete.

Pete turned his back to him and hunched over.

"Pete?"

"Sorry, Benny. I'm sorry."

"Don't worry about it," said Benny forcing a laugh. "It's been a tough day, right?"

Pete remained silent.

"Let Maggie have a look at your arm, Pete"

Still no response from Pete.

"Pete?"

Benny gently put his hand on Pete's shoulder and gave it the slightest of shakes. Pete turned his head slowly and looked at Benny.

Pete's eyes were red.

Chapter 11

"Holy shit! Everyone get back!" yelled Benny.

"Stacey, get out!" shouted Arnold as he jumped forward, grabbed Pete by the throat with both hands and pinned him up against the mantelpiece. Pete opened his mouth and snapped at Arnold's wrists.

"Maggie, go!" shouted Benny.

"I got him, I got him," said Arnold, restraining Pete.

"Just hold him there," said Maggie, who left to go into the kitchen.

"Wait! You're not going to get the shotgun are you?" said Benny as he followed her.

"Don't take too long, whatever you do," shouted Arnold, as he was left alone with Pete.

"No, I'm not going to shoot him," said Maggie as she walked over to a cupboard. "That would make too much of a mess in my sitting room."

"What's going on?" asked Beth as she sat with Kerry still on her lap.

"Pete's turned," said Benny. "What are you doing, Maggie?"

"Here, take this," said Maggie as she handed Benny a thick brown rope. "I know you don't want to hurt your friend but we have to do something about him."

"At least you're not shooting him, I guess," said Benny taking the rope and dashing back into the living room.

"What you got there?" said Arnold panicky. "He's nearly bit my finger off!"

"Some rope. Now, what's the best way to do this?" wondered Benny out loud

"Just do it quick, whatever you're going to do," shouted Arnold as he continued to struggle restraining Pete.

"Put this on his head," said Maggie returning to the living room, carrying an old black motorcycle helmet.

Benny immediately dropped the rope and took the helmet off her. He turned it backwards and placed it on top of Pete's head. "Just watch your fingers," he said as he began sliding down over Pete's head. Once Benny had gotten the helmet down half way, Arnold let go off Pete and then helped shoved it on the full way. They both stood back and watched as the now defanged Pete aimlessly walked around the living room.

"That's that taken care off," said Arnold sidestepping Pete and then giving him a vicious shove.

Pete fell forward to the floor and before his rabid mind knew what was happening Arnold pinned him to the floor with one foot.

"Not too hard, Arn," shouted Benny as he knelt down and tied a noose around Pete's ankles. "Maybe there's a cure or something."

"Maybe," said Arnold as he watched Benny finish tying up Pete's feet. "So where you plan on keeping him then? You got a basement here?"

"Best to take him outside and tie him to the big tree out there," said Maggie. "Can you drag him out?"

"Yeah, no problem. I've got this," said Benny giving the rope a strong yank. He pulled Pete through the living room, into the hall and then into the kitchen.

"What the hell are you doing?" shrieked Stacey.

Beth held Kerry's hand and with her own free hand gently pulled Stacey back to the corner of the kitchen.

"Just let them through," she said doing her best to sound calm.

"That tree over there," said Maggie holding the kitchen door open and pointing to the outside.

Benny dragged Pete out the kitchen door and across the yard.

"Sorry about this, old pal," sighed Benny as tied the other end of the rope around the tree. Maggie came along behind him and inspected the knot as Pete rolled around in the dirt making gargling noises from underneath the helmet.

"Not bad, young man," she said. "That should hold your friend for a bit."

"You think he can be cured?" asked Benny sadly.

Maggie put her arm around Benny as she walked him back to the house.

"I don't know, Benny. I think the important thing is to get you inside, washed, fed and rested. Then we'll think about what to do next."

"Should somebody stay out here and watch Pete?"

"He'll be fine. If it rains I'll put a blanket over him.

Despite Maggie's pleas, Benny remained at the kitchen door, staring out blankly towards his tied up friend. He remained deep in thought for hours as he tried to come to terms that in the same day not only has he lost his brother but he has also potentially lost his best friend too. The two closest people to him in the world are now gone leaving him behind in a very different world.

"It's not going to do you any good standing there all day, Benny," said Beth.

"I know," said Benny softly. "I'm just thinking how I'm going to tell my parents about Jason. And then I'll have to tell Pete's folks as well."

Beth walked over and put her arms round Benny and held him close. She was lost for words. She knew nothing she could say would make Benny feel even remotely better.

"You should lie down for a bit," she said eventually. "You're not going to be much use to us if you're exhausted."

"I haven't been much use anyway," he muttered.

"Don't say that," she said firmly. "I would have been run over this morning if it hadn't been for you."

"I'm sure you would have moved in time anyway."

"Bullshit!" she said, raising the tone in her voice. "And you certainly helped us get through that town alive."

"That was mostly Arnold, to be fair."

"Thanks, Benny," came Arnold's voice. They both turned around to see him standing at the doorway to the kitchen. "And don't be so modest, man. You were pretty tough there when that fat bastard was on top of me."

"Who was on top of you?" asked Beth confused.

"That big guy in the shop where we found Kerry. I thought I was a goner there." Arnold leaned over and gave Benny a gentle punch on the arm.

"Anytime, Arn."

"Well, now that you two are now best friends for life, how about you go get some rest, Benny?" said Beth. "There's a spare room at the top of the stairs on the left. Go on."

"Better do what she says, Benny," said Arnold. "I'll keep an eye on Pete."

Benny looked over to Beth as if to protest but once he looked at her he realised he couldn't bring himself to argue with her.

"Maybe an hour or so wouldn't hurt," he said as he slowly walked towards the hall. He turned around when he got to the door.

"You'll tell me if anything happens, will you?"

"Of course we will, Benny. Now go get some rest," said Beth pointing in the direction of the hall. "Go on. Don't make me say it again."

Arnold sat up on the kitchen bench and quietly laughed.

"What?" said Beth.

"Nothing, nothing," he said trying to stifle a laugh.

"Somebody has to look after you boys," she said, jokingly.

The smile slowly disappeared from Arnold's face.

"Yeah, I know. Thanks for everything."

Arnold looked down and took a deep breath.

"What's up?" she asked.

"I don't know," he mumbled.

Beth leaned over and put her arm around him.

"You hang in there. You're doing a good job keeping us all safe. An excellent job."

Arnold looked at her and forced a small smile.

"Yeah, thanks. I just wish Jason was still with us."

"Me too."

"So you finally convinced that young man to get some rest?"

Maggie walked in and sat down at the kitchen table.

"Sorry, I hope I'm not interrupting something here."

"Oh no, it's nothing like that," said Beth quickly removing her arm from Arnold.

"Er, yeah," said Arnold with a hint of disappointment in his voice.

"Is Stacey still upstairs?" asked Beth.

"Yes, she's helping give Kerry a bath. Thought you could do with a small break from looking after her. Young girls can be so tiring."

"I don't mind, really. She's a lovely girl."

"Yes, she certainly is," said Maggie. "I dread to think what sort of world she's going to be growing up in. Even if this mess is every sorted."

Beth walked over to the table, pulled out a seat and sat down beside Maggie.

"What do you think has happened," she asked.

Maggie looked behind her towards the door, then turned back to look at Beth. Arnold then joined them at the table sitting beside Beth.

"I didn't want to say with Kerry about earlier. God knows, she must be frightened enough."

"I think we've all had quite a frightening time," said Beth.

"Well, you'll be safe in here, Beth," said Maggie gently patting Beth's arm. "It wasn't safe out there this morning and it certainly isn't going to be any safer at night."

"I'm surprised the army or the police haven't been through yet," said Arnold. "What's taking them so long?"

"They're either very busy…" said Maggie.

"Or?" asked Arnold.

"There is none."

"That can't be true! They've got to do something." he exclaimed.

"Well, as much as I wish for it, I'm not so filled with confidence," said Maggie as she leaned back in her chair. "I was round at my friend Cathy's house this morning when all this madness began. We were just having our weekly coffee morning just like we do every Friday and we were just waiting for everyone else to arrive."

Maggie leaned forward and rested her head in her hands as she thought. "When I think back, I think there was a new report on the television. Some volcano had just erupted. I can't remember which one or what country it even was in. They were just about to cut to an on the spot reporter, when the picture just went black. We didn't think much at first because you know what it's like with television programs and things going wrong. But then there was this really strange chanting."

"Chanting?" said Beth and Arnold together. They both looked at each other.

"Was it like the stuff being said on the radio?" asked Arnold.

"I don't really know what it is to be honest," continued Maggie. "It was strange. Evil sounding. I dare not even turn my own television on in case it's still playing."

"Benny said it was on the phone as well," said Beth. "What can it mean?"

"Cathy didn't like it, whatever it was," said Maggie. "She turned the television off just as there was knocking at the door. Not knocking like a normal person but banging. Thumping with fists. Cathy went to see who it was. A few seconds later I heard her scream out and I raced round to see what the commotion was."

Maggie gulped as she began to shake. Beth placed one arm around the old woman and held her hand with her free hand.

"It's okay. Maggie. You don't have to think about it."

Maggie looked up at Beth and smiled. "I can see why Kerry has taken to you." She squeezed Beth's hand and took a deep breath.

"It was Francis. Cathy's cousin. I don't know what happened to her but she was not right. She was hunched over Cathy and..."

"Maggie, you don't have to say any more." pleaded Beth, seeing the woman's eyes start to water.

"I couldn't do anything. It was too late. Francis had killed Cathy in one of the most heinous ways possible. I fled the house as fast as I could. It was madness. People who were once my good friends had the devil's eyes in them."

"It freaks the hell out of me too." said Arnold.

"It took me forever to get back to my house safely. Cathy's house isn't too far away, but I'm not as young as I once was. I had to avoid and hide from almost a dozen of them before I got home. I got the shotgun out as soon as I did. You must have arrived less than fifteen minutes later."

"You think we're still safe here?" said Beth. "We're grateful you've given us sanctuary from out there, but you said you encountered how many on your way to here."

"A dozen," she replied solemnly. "They don't move too fast so we should be able to spot any of them coming up."

"It's going to start getting dark soon," said Arnold getting up. "I think we should keep the lights off and move upstairs. I'll keep a watch out from the windows."

"Hopefully if any of those things come this way, we'll stay unnoticed and they'll walk on by," said Beth.

"That's what I'm hoping too. I better make sure the all doors are all locked and secured," said Arnold as he disappeared into the hall.

"You think Pete is going to be alright out there," said Beth as she got up and looked at him out the window.

"I believe so," said Maggie getting up also. "They don't attack each other so I think in that respect he is safe. We better go upstairs now. Arnold is right. It will be dark soon."

"What does blondes have more fun mean?"

"Hmm?" replied Stacey as she continued brushing Kerry's hair.

"Do they have more fun?"

"Where on earth did you hear that?" laughed Stacey.

"I'm not having fun and I'm blonde."

"Yeah, it's not much fun for any of us today," said Stacey.

"Do you have fun?"

"What do you mean?" said Stacey, putting the brush down on the bedside cabinet.

"Well, you're blonde. Does that mean you have more fun? Do people like you more?"

"You ask a lot of difficult questions for a little kid," said Stacey nervously.

"Beth isn't blonde but I bet everyone likes her. I like her lots. She's nice."

"I think it's time for you to get some sleep. It's been... quite a day." said Stacey as she pulled back the bed covers for Kerry.

"Will I see my mummy and daddy tomorrow?" said Kerry as she jumped onto the bed.

Stacey smiled dryly.

"I think I preferred the questions about blondes."

Benny lay on the bed but was far from feeling sleepy. He knew he needed to rest but his mind kept alternating between Jason's final moments and Pete before he turned. Then he worried about how he was going to keep Beth, Kerry, Stacy and Maggie all safe. He couldn't leave it all to Arnold. Arnold may not be acting the selfish jerk that he normally is but he's no Jason. He showed signs of cracking a couple of times earlier.

"Trouble sleeping?"

Benny turned to see Arnold standing at the doorway.

"Yeah," mumbled Benny. "Can't really relax in a new place at the best of times."

Arnold walked into the room and stood at the window.

"That makes two of us," said Arnold leaning on the window frame and stared out. "I hope to God a police car or something turns up and tells us everything's been sorted. We can go back home and carry on as before."

"Even if that did happen, it'll never be the same again," said Benny sadly.

"Yeah..."

"Arnold?"

"Yeah, Ben?"

"What do we do? Do we just wait here?"

"I guess. Somebody's bound to come and get us. They have to."

"You don't think, maybe we're the last ones?" said Benny sitting up from the bed.

Arnold looked over at Benny nervously then quickly looked back out the window.

"No, of course not. You're nearly as bad as Maggie. There's others like us out there. The government probably has a whole team and people who knew this was going to happen. We'll be fine."

"Yeah, we'll be fine," said Benny lying back down in bed not convinced one iota that Arnold was sure of what he was saying.

"Benny! Get up! Now!" whispered Arnold.

"What's wrong?" said Benny shooting straight up.

"Where are the others?"

"Think I hear Beth and Maggie coming up the stairs and I think Stacey and Kerry are in the bedroom. What's up?"

"Look!"

Benny dashed over to the window and looked out. There were six red eyes heading up the driveway towards the house. They were different this time. They weren't stumbling, brainless goofs. They were walking quickly and confidently towards them.

"Shit!" hissed Benny as he turned to Arnold." Do they know we're here?"

Arnold said nothing as he dashed from the window and out to the hall were Beth and Maggie were. He quickly ushered them into the bedroom where Kerry and Stacey were.

Benny looked back to the window and saw that the red eyes were now much closer. All six of them were grown men. Big men as well who were looking directly up at Benny's window. Benny noticed something different about them. It was their eyes. They weren't just red but they were glowing. Like a pair of red lights.

Then Benny heard them all speaking together, repeating the same phrase over and over again. He struggled to make it out at first but then it hit him.

"Waaan Theee Zerro Kay Zerro Aree!"

Chapter 12

Benny ran out into the hall where Arnold was waiting for him.
"They know we're here!" he shouted. "It's my fault! They saw
me!"

"Shit!" muttered Arnold. "Okay, we've been in worse! We can
do this!"

"They only saw me! You guys hide and I'll draw them away
from the house!"

"You've been taking too many hero pills, kid," said Arnold as
he took Benny by the arm and led him into the room where the
girls were in.

"What's going on?" said Stacey. "How many of them are
outside?"

"Only a few," said Arnold closing the door. "Five? Maybe six."

"We can deal with that, surely?" said Beth. "You did lock the
doors downstairs, didn't you, Arnold?"

A loud crash consisting of broken glass and breaking wood was
heard from down below.

"Well, I did."

"Are we going to jump out a window again?" said Stacey
looking nervously towards the bedroom window.

"That's far too high. That's just suicide," said Maggie.

"She's right," said Benny looking out the window. "It's higher
up and I can see two more of those things down there."

"I hear them coming up the stairs," said Arnold as he dragged a
chest of drawers across the door. "They move fast!"

"The bed too," shouted Benny as he pushed it out from the wall. Stacey and Beth then helped him move it so it was up against the chest of drawers.

"This is all looking very familiar," said Benny. "Didn't we do this recently?"

"Yeah but this time we have this beauty," said Arnold pointing at Maggie.

"Excuse me?" gasped Maggie.

"I meant the gun!"

"Oh, yes, I see" said Maggie looking down at the shotgun in her hands.

"Waaan Theee Zerro Kay Zerro Aree!"

"They're here," shouted Arnold. "Blow a hole through the door!"

"Wait!" yelled Benny. "You can't just shoot at the door. That's holding them back."

"And the gun's not loaded either," said Maggie.

"What?" said Arnold.

"I never keep it loaded. It's too dangerous especially with Kerry about."

An array of fists began to beat down upon the bedroom door as the bizarre chant became louder.

"Waaan Theee Zerro Kay Zerro Aree!"

"That door isn't going to hold these ones," said Beth scooping Kerry up in her arms.

Without needing to communicate with each other Benny and Arnold both ran over to a large wardrobe and together pushed it so it joined the barricade made up of the bed and cabinet.

"Now what?" said Stacey.

"The attic," said Kerry pointing up to a trap door leading to the roof space.

"Good girl," said Beth. "Guys, can you get us all up there?"

Arnold jumped up onto the bed and pushed the wooden panel up and over.

"You get up there first," said Benny. "I'll help get people up and you get them in."

Arnold reached up and with ease pulled himself up into the attic roof space. He turned around and put his hands out to take the first person. Benny grabbed Kerry from Beth and handed her up to Arnold before the little girl had time to protest.

"You next, Maggie," said Beth.

Benny lifted her up by below the waist and once again Arnold reached down and pulled her up.

"Hurry, guys!" shouted Arnold as he noticed the banging became louder as was the sound of the door wood splitting.

"Go, Stacey," said Beth as she pushed her towards Benny. Like with Maggie, he lifted her up towards Arnold who quickly pulled her up.

"Me next," said Beth as she pulled herself close to Benny and smiled.

Benny smiled nervously and took a hold of Beth and raised her up. Just as Arnold grabbed her, the bed that they had been standing on shot out several feet.

"Shit!" shouted Benny as he found himself lying on the floor. He looked up to see Beth being dragged up into the roof space by both Arnold and Stacey.

"Come on, Benny!" yelled out Arnold, holding out his hand. Benny looked over to see part of the door to bedroom had been broken away and behind the blockage of the cabinet and wardrobe, stood a tall man with red glowing eyes. He reached around the wardrobe and began pushing it away.

"Benny, you got to move now!" screamed Beth.

Benny shot up and ran towards the bed. He put one foot on the bed post and launched himself towards Arnold's outreached hand.

"I got you! I got you!"

Arnold frantically reeled Benny in, just pulling him out of reach as the red eye dived towards him.

"They're not supposed to move that fast!" gasped Benny as he looked back down.

The room below soon filled up with three others, all of them with the same glowing red eyes. They looked straight up at the group in the attic, snarling and reaching for them. They still continued with the sinister chant.

"Waaan Theee Zerro Kay Zerro Aree!"

"Waaan Theee Zerro Kay Zerro Aree!"

"Waaan Theee Zerro Kay Zerro Aree!"

"I'm sick of hearing that," said Benny as he pushed the square piece of wood over the hole.

The attic was dark with a lonely bay window at the far end letting the dusk light in.

"Can we block this up?" said Stacey.

"We should be safe," said Arnold. "They're thick as shit."

"No!" shouted Benny. "These ones are different. They're not as brainless as the other ones! They'll get up here eventually!"

"Push this over," said Maggie pointing over to a large trunk.

Arnold grabbed it by the handle and pulled it over the trapdoor. Down below he could make out the sound of further commotion in the bedroom. It seemed Benny was right. They were working out a way of getting to them.

"This isn't going to be as easy as getting out of the shop," said Arnold.

"That doesn't help us, Arnold," said Beth annoyed. "We need to think fast."

Benny raced across the dusty floor to the window. He opened it and looked outside.

"Too far to jump," he muttered. "But maybe…"

"What you thinking, Benny?" asked Stacey.

"You got the car keys, Arnold?" said Benny.

"Er, yeah. Why?"

"This might sound crazy, but I think if I can get down to the ground and get to the car, I might be able to lure them all away from here. Then I can double back, pick you all up and we can get the hell away from here."

"You're crazy," said Arnold. "Absolutely bat shit crazy."

"We don't have any choice. If I don't make it, you'll have to come up with another plan. But right now, this is all I got."

Arnold thought for a brief moment. He knew it was suicide but at this precise moment he couldn't think of anything else.

"Alright, Ben," he said fishing the keys out of his pocket and throwing them towards Benny.

"Arnold!" protested Beth. She then turned to Benny who was halfway out the window. "Benny, you can't do this! It's too dangerous!"

Benny never answered Beth as he stepped out onto the narrow ledge outside the attic window. Slowly he edged along it until he was able to climb onto the roof.

"Be careful," cried out Beth which was just about audible to Benny. He stood up the best he could and carefully ran up towards the peak of the roof. He looked around still unsure how he was going to put his bravado plan into action. Sliding down a drain pipe to freedom might sound good in theory but the reality of it made him realise it may not be quite as easy. As quickly as he possibly could without endangering himself, Benny made his way to the end of the roof. Two stories was far too big a drop to be practical but there was a one level extension to the side of the house.

He moved along the roof gingerly as he edged closer to the extension of the house. He could sense movement from below circling around the house. He hoped he had the attention of the intruders so at least part of his plan was working.

The extension was a much newer building than the main farm house, possibly added within the last twenty years. Benny lowered himself from the edge of the roof, remembering how Arnold had done earlier in the day back in the town. He let go and dropped down to the lower roof. He stumbled and tumbled forward but managed to keep himself standing vertical. He looked over to the ground to his right and down below two glowing red eyes were staring up at him with their hands pointing at him. Three other red eyes ran out from the house and joined the two pointing out Benny.

"Waaan Theee Zerro Kay Zerro Aree!"

Benny looked over his shoulder to the other side of the building and saw that it seemed clear of red eyes. He moved as quickly as he could to the far side and dropped down to the ground below. He stumbled and fell over.

"Shit!"

The red eyes on the far side of the building let out a howl. Benny then heard them running round the house.

"Aw shit! Shit! Shit!"

He started to run. He looked over his shoulder and saw several of the new improved red eyes appearing from around the corner of the house. They were following behind him and they were fast. His father's car came into his view and put his hand in his pocket to pull out the key.

"Aw shit! Shit! Shit!"

He couldn't find it. He reached the car and still no luck in finding the key. He turned around, knowing full well, that the red eyes were seconds away to killing him. The six of them had stopped running and were slowly spreading out, surrounding Benny. He looked at each one in turn as they looked back at him, almost mockingly. One of them stood out to Benny. The one straight in front of him. It was Pete.

"Pete! Listen to me! You got to fight this!"

Pete raised his head up and spoke.

"Waaan Theee Zerro Kay Zerro Aree!"

"What does that mean? Come on Pete"

The other red eyes joined in with chant and closed in on Benny. Benny closed his eyes and prepared to die.

A gun shot rang out.

Benny opened his eyes to see Pete, with half his head missing drop to the ground. He turned around to see two shadowy figures. The larger figure held what appeared to be two sawn off shotguns while the leaner one held a hand gun.

"Better get down, son," said the one with the hand gun taking aim.

Benny dived to the ground for cover as the two figures fired a blast of gun shots. He looked up when the firing stopped to see the red eyes lying on the ground, mostly with parts of their heads missing.

"W-who are you?" stammered Benny.

"We're the guys who just saved your life, son," said the larger man. Without the threat of death breathing on him, Benny was able to take a better look at his saviours. The larger man looked to Benny like a stereotypical Hell Angels biker. Dressed in grubby denim and a sleeveless Hawkwind t-shirt, he had endless tattoos on both arms and a patronising sneer on his bald bearded face. The other man, who wore a white shirt with a black tie and trousers, had a very calm and collected mood about him. He was quite a contrast to his companion.

"You killed my friend," said Benny sadly. The biker man gave out a sickening chuckle.

"Stop that now, Horace," said the other man. "I'm sorry, but you friend was long gone. We had to do what we did."

Benny looked down at the body of his friend. The man walked up behind Benny put his hand on his shoulder.

"I know it doesn't feel like it now, but what we did was for the best for him. The others too."

Benny remained silent. He looked up to see Horace reloading one of the shot guns while holding the other one between his legs. He swapped the guns positions, and reloaded the other.

"Hey, Tom. I'm gonna check around the house for more of them freaky bastards," said Horace.

Tom pulled out a black plastic box, about the size of a walkie talkie and examined the display of dials.

"Should be fine," he called over. "But just be careful, there might be a few it didn't pick up."

Horace walked off towards the back of the house shouting expletives with every step he took.

"He's not so bad when you get to know him," said Tom.

"There's worse souls than him."

"Who..What..who are you? What's going on?" said Benny, still trying to take in what happened.

"There's time for explanations when we get you back. What's your name?"

"Er, Benny."

Are you on your own then, Benny?"

"No. My friends are still up in the attic."

"How many?"

"Six. Well six if you count me."

"Good. Well let's go get them and get you all back to base safe. You've nothing to worry about now, Benny. Everything's going to be fine for you and your friends. Trust me."

"Thanks," said Benny, "I just hope this is the end of it."

Little did Benny know, his and his friends problems, were far from over.

Chapter 13

"Six people? Looks like it was worthwhile checking this place out then," said a man who could have passed for Horace's fatter and older brother. He leaned against a bus that was parked at the bottom of the drive to Maggie's house while holding tight a shotgun.

"Certainly was, Frankie," said Horace with a smug look on his face. "Must have taken out ten of them in one go."

"You lying bastard," laughed Frankie. "Well, you good folks all get aboard the fun bus."

He stepped aside and pointed to the bus door with his gun.

"Where are we going," asked Stacey nervously.

"Somewhere safe, my sweet thing," said Frankie with a toothless smile across his face. "Don't worry, I'm here to keep you safe."

Stacey shuddered as she stepped onto the bus.

"Ah, a pretty blonde and a pretty non blonde," said the driver who could have been Frankie's fatter and older brother.

Stacey and Beth both put their heads down and avoided eye contact as they passed him. They sat down together on a seat in front of a worried looking woman with a young boy about eight years old, sitting on her lap.

Maggie and Kerry were next to get on the bus. The driver politely nodded to them although it still remained creepy as well. Maggie did her best to smile back despite him making her feel very uneasy.

"Mummy!" shouted Kerry, as she ran down the bus towards the woman sitting behind Beth and Stacey.

The woman broke out of her worried trance and let out a shriek of joy.

"Kerry! Oh thank God," she said as she wrapped her arms around Kerry and her son at the same time. "I thought I lost you."

"Laura! Eddie!" shouted Maggie as she ran down to join them.

"Mum! You're alive too," said Laura as tears flowed down her face.

"Yes, thanks, to these young people," she said as she sat down on the seat beside her daughter and grandchildren. "We wouldn't be alive it wasn't for them,"

Laura looked at with a large smile on her face and unable to speak due to the emotions, mouthed the words 'thank you.'

"Now you two little boys don't be worrying. We'll take good care of you and those nice girlfriends of yours," said Horace as Benny and Arnold both boarded the bus. Benny turned and glared at Horace but Arnold gently pushed him along.

"Now, Horace," said Tom from behind. "I hope you're not giving these two men any bother. I won't have any of it."

"Not at all, Tom. Wouldn't dream of it," laughed Horace.

"There's a good man," replied Tom. "Think we've done all we can tonight. We've lost a few already. Wouldn't want to lose the rest of you. Take us back home, Jonesy."

"You got it," said the driver, who as soon as Tom, Horace and Frankie got on board, closed the door and started the bus off down the road.

Benny and Arnold sat on a bench across from Beth and Stacey. While the girls were occupied with talking to Kerry's mother, the two of them were given time to look around at the other passengers on the bus.

Two seats behind where Laura was sitting, was a young teenage couple, both looking absolutely terrified as they held each other in their arms.

Behind them was an elderly priest who kept his head down and mumbled what sounded like a prayer over and over again while crossing himself. Along the back row seats slept a down and out man with his back to the rest of the bus. The smell of alcohol coming from him told Benny and Arnold that perhaps it wasn't tiredness that was the cause of his sleeping.

The last passenger on the bus was an excitable young man, barely out of his teens. He wore a sweater with the hood up and a leather jacket over that. He spied Benny looking around at everyone and slid from his seat to the one behind Benny and Arnold.

"What a crazy day this turned out to be," he said removing a packet of crisps from his pocket and then stuffed a handful into his mouth. He held it out to Benny and Arnold who both politely shock their heads.

"Suit yourselves," he said taking another handful. "Connor."

"What?" said Benny.

"My name's Connor."

"Benny," said Benny. "This is Arnold."

"Those lot with you as well," said Connor pointing over to Beth and Stacey.

"Yeah," said Arnold. "We had another two, but they didn't make it."

"Yeah, I used to have a lot of friends too until today," said Connor. "Not too sure how many I have left now. Maybe none."

"What the hell has happened?" asked Benny.

"That's the big question isn't it?" said Connor before pouring the remaining contents of the crisp packet down his throat. "I haven't a clue is my answer. There I was working in my uncle's warehouse then the next minute he comes out with blood all over his face. It wasn't just him. Seemed like everyone was either eating or being eaten. I legged it like a bastard."

"So who are these guys here," said Arnold nodding over towards Tom and the brothers sitting at the front end of the bus.

Connor leaned over closer and lowered his voice

"Well you see the guy in the shirt and tie? He's Thomas Casson. According to a guy who was on this bus, he runs this religious retreat place somewhere out in the country. That's where they're taking us now. Apparently it's the safest place in five hundred miles."

"Wait a minute," said Arnold. "What do you mean by a guy who was on the bus? Where is he now?"

"Well it seems the wise and all knowing Tommy Casson didn't realise that the crazy folks with the bloody eyes went a little bit crazier when the sun starts to go down. There used to be a few more people on here before we picked you up."

"So that's what happened to Pete then," said Benny.

"Pete? He was one of your friends?" said Connor. "I take it he changed, and then changed again?"

"Yeah, something like that," replied Benny.

"And what about the three stooges then?" said Arnold.

"I don't know much about them. Seem like the sort of people your parents told you to stay away from and here we are now, on their bus being taken to their home."

"You think they belong to this religious retreat group?" asked Arnold.

"You think they look like God squad?" laughed Connor.

"No, but then, I guess you can be surprised what people are like underneath it all," replied Arnold.

"True," said Connor. "I guess not."

"What's that thing Tom's got?" asked Benny. "I saw him looking at it when we got on the bus."

"From what I gather, it seems to be able to detect if any of those things are near. Didn't work quite so well whenever we lost a few people but then that was before we knew what happened when it got dark."

"So they don't quite know everything then," stated Arnold.

"Well yes and no," said Connor, moving even closer to the two in front. "This is what's been bothering me. This whole thing kicked off this morning, right?"

"Yeah," agreed Arnold.

"It seems to have caught the army and police by surprise," continued Connor. "I haven't seen or heard any of them coming along and saving the day."

"We were hoping they'd be the ones turning up at our door, telling us it will be okay," said Benny.

"Exactly!" said Connor. "No army or nothing but these guys instead. How come the government with all their so called intelligence and experts and all that shit, didn't see this coming, but these guys did and they are now the heroes?"

Benny and Arnold looked at each other bewildered, both realising that the strange man who approached them on the bus, actually had a very good point.

"So this guy Tom is the saviour of the universe?" said Arnold.

"Well I wouldn't go that far. I don't think he's the head of it all. From what I gather he's answering to someone else. He's got a walkie-talkie in his pocket along with that other device. Couldn't tell you who though. They like to keep their cards close to their chests."

"So they've been driving round picking up survivors?" said Benny.

"Not just survivors, they've been picking up loads of supplies and stuff. Food, drink, batteries, anything useful. The usual shit you'd want to pick up in your standard run of the mill end of the world situation."

"Hey!" yelled Horace from the front of the bus. "Hope you're not talking shit with them two boys!"

"Of course not!" shouted back Connor. "Just participating in the art of social interaction! You should give it a go sometime!"

Horace simply snorted and turned back around.

"Fool," muttered Connor. "Hard to believe these are the guys with their shit together."

Horace turned around again and stared at Connor, not hearing what he was saying but knowing it was about him. Connor cheekily smiled back and waved causing Horace to shake his head.

"Still, they mustn't have been totally expecting it otherwise they would had more food and shit already gathered up. According to the guy who was eaten earlier, they found an army truck that had crashed along one of the roads."

"An army truck?" said Benny, thinking back to what both Pete and Beth had told him earlier in the day.

"Yeah," said Connor, looking up towards Horace then once again leaning closer towards the two. "They found a few guns and something else."

"Something else? Like what?" asked Benny.

"I don't know."

"Interesting," said Arnold sarcastically.

"No seriously," said Connor agitated. "The guy who's name I wish to God I could remember said they definitely found something really important."

"But you don't know what it is?" said Arnold.

"No."

"Do you know what it even looks like?" asked Benny.

"No, they picked it up before they found me but listen, whatever it is, that guy told me it's in the overhead locker above were the driver is sitting. Everything else they find they just shove it in the normal luggage compartment. Even the guns. So what's so important that they keep it that close?"

Benny and Arnold looked at each, both wondering what to really make of Connor who then leaned back in his seat, put his hands behind his head and sighed.

"Then again, I would have been dead if these guys hadn't come along so I probably should just let things go, you know?"

"Yeah I guess we'd be dead too," said Benny, looking over towards Beth and the other. "As would everyone on this bus, I imagine."

Beth looked up from her group conversation and smiled over at him. It was the sort of smile that said we're going to be okay even though things were going to be very different.

"They your girlfriends or something" asked Connor.

Benny paused. He knew the answer was no, but something about saying no made him feel a bit sad. Maybe it was because he lost both his brother and his best friend on the same day made him feel lonely and admitting he didn't have a girlfriend just made it seem worse.

"They're with us," said Arnold.

"That's cool, just asking. No problem, friend?"

"Look alive, gentlemen. We've got trouble coming," said Tom loudly as he stood up, gazing at his strange device that had begun to beep.

"Excellent," laughed Horace brandishing his guns. "Bring on the fun!"

Chapter 14

"Keep your speed up," said Tom, pulling out his handgun. "This thing's going off the scale."

He placed the device on the dashboard of the bus and lifted a second handgun from the overhead compartment above his seat.

"How many you reckon?" said Jonesy, looking frantically.

"Lots," replied Tom. He turned around to face the passengers of the bus.

"Can I have your attention, people," he announced. "Things are going to get a little lively here, but just keep your heads down and keep calm. We'll get you back safe. I promise."

"Shit!" shouted Jonesy. "Up ahead!"

Tom looked up and saw a group of ten red eyes running fearlessly along the road straight towards the bus.

"Speed up and aim for the side of the group," ordered Tom. "Everyone, hang on!"

Jonesy pressed hard on the accelerator pedal and just as he approached the group he turned slightly to the right. He missed the bulk of the group but taking two of the red eyes out. The first one bounced off the side of the bus while the next one was crunched underneath the front wheel of the bus.

"Alright!" cheered Horace as the bus shook, "That's the way to sort the bastards out!"

"Sure is," laughed Frankie, turning around to the other passengers. "You see that? That's how you deal with them lot!"

"Reel it in, men," said Tom sternly. "We're not out of it yet."
Out to the sides of the road scores of red eyes were sprinting towards the bus as it passed by them. The bus, traveling too fast for any of them to catch it, still felt the occasional bump as several red eyes were able to just connect with it.

"They're really starting to move now," said Frankie, as he aimed his shotgun out the window. "Easier when they didn't move just as fast."

"Don't be firing off just yet," said Tom. "They're not causing us any trouble yet. As long as Jonesy can get us past them, we hold off."

"Awww, boss," said Frankie.

"Save the ammo, Frank. If the road gets too blocked for Jonesy to drive through we're going to have to clear it quick."

"You could pass a gun or two down this way if you'd like," shouted Connor from the back.

"I wouldn't give you a toothbrush," barked Horace.

"Well if you had one I'd rather you keep it yourself." called back Connor.

"And I thought Pete was annoying," muttered Arnold.

Before Horace could respond to Connor's insult, a large thud was heard from the roof, as if something human sized had landed on it.

"That can't be?" said Benny.

Tom dashed to the back were the sound came from and fired several shots with both guns into the roof. He stopped and from the back window watched as a human sized shape rolled off and fell to the ground below.

"The darker it gets, the more dangerous these things get it seems," said Tom.

"There's more of them up ahead!" shouted Jonesy. "A lot more!"

Everyone looked up ahead to see a huge mob of red eyes on the road running straight for the bus.

"Thankfully they're still lacking in intelligence and reason," said Tom, making his way back to the driver. "Ram them!"

Jonesy drove into the side of the group just like before but this time was unable to avoid hitting quite a few of them. The bus bounced up and to the side as it collided with each red eye.

"Jesus! Mary! Joseph! Judas!" exclaimed Jonesy as he struggled to keep control of the bus.

"Keep going!" shouting Tom as he grabbed the wheel and helped Jonesy keep the steering straight. "Keep driving through and less of the blasphemy!"

Thuds were heard all around the bus as it continued to plough through the group of red eyes. The familiar chant from them began to echo all around.

"You know what that means?" Benny said to Connor.

"Haven't a clue. You?"

Without warning, the window panel beside Beth and Stacey cracked into pixilated blue fragments, causing both girls to grab each other. Benny dashed from his seat towards them and pulled them both to the opposite side of the bus.

"Now you're going to get it, you bastards," said Horace

storming down to the damaged window. With the butt of one of his shotguns he knocked the glass out of the frame and stuck both guns out the window. He fired both guns twice as he laughed insanely.

"Horace!" yelled Tom angrily. "What are you doing, you fool?"

Horace turned towards Tom but before he could a young red eye woman sprung up from below the bus and hung on the window frame. She reached over, grabbed Horace by the arm and pulled him across to the window causing him to drop both guns outside.

"You bitch!" screamed Horace as she sunk her teeth into his arm.

Beth raced up and took a hold of Horace's belt and tried to pull him in. Just as Tom ran down and reached Horace himself, a second red eye woman, appeared at the window and grabbed Horace firmly by the throat.

Tom fired a shot each to the heads of the two red eyes. Both of them fell to the ground and disappeared from sight. Horace stumbled back and landed on a seat opposite.

"Oh my God!" gasped Stacey as she saw the front of Horace was covered in blood as he was gasping for breath. "His throat! His throat's been ripped out!"

"Horace!" cried Frankie, who dropped his shot gun and cradled Horace in his arms, not caring or realising that he was getting himself covered in blood.

"Do something for him! Please!" pleaded Frankie.

"First, you pick up that shot gun and guard that window," said Tom to Benny. "Shoot anything that tries to come through."

"Me?" said Benny, reluctantly picking up the gun. "How do I..."

The bus continued to bump along as Tom took a closer look at Horace's injuries.

"He's going to be alright, isn't he?" shouted a desperate Frankie.

Horace stared vacantly back at Tom as he gurgled and wheezed blood from the new hole in his throat.

"I'm sorry," he said, bringing his gun to Horace's temple.

"No!" shouted Frankie, Beth, Stacey, Arnold, Benny, Maggie, Laura, the praying priest and the young couple at the back.

"We can't save him! We have to end his suffering!"

Tom pulled the trigger as everyone clenched their eyes tight and looked away. Horace sharply flinched and then was still.

"Oh God!" sobbed Frankie as he clutched Horace's lifeless bloody body.

"There was nothing we could do for him, Frank. I'm sorry," said Tom as he handed both guns to Stacey. "Hold these for a moment."

He took hold of Horace's body in a bear hug and then wrenched it up from Frankie's embrace. He then spun round and shoved Horace's body out the window.

The body had barely hit the ground when it was pounced upon by several red eyes. This caught the attention of several others along the road who turned their attention away from the passing bus and dived into the swarm to join in the feast.

Frankie yelled out a wail of sorrow while everyone else looked at Tom in shock who calmly took the two guns of a dumbfounded Stacy.

"That was very difficult for me," said Tom, looking down to see his once white shirt was now mostly red. "But believe me, we had no choice."

"You bastard! How could you?" screamed Frankie, getting up and making a move towards Tom. He stopped dead when Tom had both guns pointed directly at his head.

"I know you're angry, Frank. Horace was my friend too. But he was going to die in a lot of pain. This was kinder for him, trust me. You wouldn't have wanted him to suffer, would you?"

Frankie closed his eyes tight as the tears flowed down his face and let out a pitiful howl. He opened them again and wiped his face with the back of his hand.

"You know I'm right, Frank," said Tom looking Frankie straight in the eye. "We had to end his pain."

"Gimme my gun," he snarled as he snatched the shotgun from Benny. "I owe them bastards something."

"Good," said Tom lowering both his guns and stepping aside to allow Frankie access to the window. "Horace will not have died in vain."

The bus continued driving down the road with the red eyes number becoming smaller and smaller. The windscreen at the front was smeared with blood and bits of flesh which unfortunately couldn't be washed away due to the wipers being missing.

"How can you see through that," called Connor from the back. "I don't want you killing us in a bus crash after surviving them whackos."

"Will you just shut your mouth?" scoffed Jonesy. "I can see just fine."

As soon as Jonesy said that, the bus suddenly jolted back and then began to veer to the right.

"Shit!" shouted Jonesy, as he braked hard and flinging his passengers about in the process. The bus then came to a stop.

"What happened?" shouted Tom, picking himself and his guns up from the floor.

"Must have hit something and whatever it is I think it's blocking the wheel," shouted Jonesy. "We got to remove it or we're not moving anywhere."

"Frank, with me now," shouted Tom as he hit a switch in front of Jonesy which opened the bus door, "Everyone else stay aboard!"

Without saying a word Frankie followed Tom outside and to the front wheel of the bus.

"Where the hell am I?"

Everyone turned around to see the gruff drunk man on the back seat had finally woken up and was now staring bewildered at all the strange faces around him.

"Oh sweet Jesus! What the hell is going on here?"

"It's okay," said Beth. "You're safe now. Please, just take it easy."

"No, I have to go! I have to get out of here!" he shouted, as he desperately looked all around him. He spied the emergency exit at the door and bolted towards it.

"Wait!" shouted Beth but it was too late. He had pulled the latch on the door and ran straight out. They heard his frantic yells stop for a split second then turn into a blood curdling scream.

"We're clear!" came Tom's voice from the front end of the bus. Everyone turned around to see both Tom and Frankie dashing back on the bus.

"Get us out of here, Jonesy!"

Without even waiting for the door to close, Jonesy put the bus into gear and drove off.

"Who was the man who ran out there?" Tom asked the passengers.

Everyone looked at each other, nobody having any idea what the man's name was.

"Whoever he was, that man bought us several precious seconds with his sacrifice," said Tom. "Those demons were distracted devouring him, giving us enough time to clear the way."

"Don't think he actually did that on purpose," said Connor. "I'm pretty sure he looked like he was going to shit himself while screaming like a madman."

"You would do well to bear in mind, young man, that we are alive because that man died," said Tom sternly. "We owe are lives to him."

"And Horace too," said a melancholy Frankie.

Tom placed his hand on Frankie's shoulder and gave it a gentle shake.

"Yes, and Horace too. I wish we could have saved him but his wounds were fatal. It's what he would have wanted."

"Yeah," muttered Frankie, not looking up.

Tom turned to address the passengers.

"Friends, it's been a difficult day for all of us. We've seen some things we'd rather not see again. But I will tell you this, you will reach sanctuary soon. There you will be safe and we will no longer lose people like we have done today. My friends, you are coming home."

Once again the passengers all looked at each other blankly none of them sure what to make of Tom and his offer.

Connor leaned over to where Benny and Arnold were now sitting.

"He's about to go ape shit," he whispered to them.

"Who?" said Arnold.

"Tom," replied Connor.

"Why's that?" asked Benny.

"You know the way I said there's something really important in the locker over there?"

Benny and Arnold both looked over towards the driver's seat and saw that the door to the locker above was open. Tom, Frankie and Jonesy obviously having not noticed yet.

"What the hell did you do?" whispered Arnold.

"I got it right here," said Connor, holding onto something underneath his jacket.

"How'd you even get that without them knowing?" asked Benny.

"I did it when that drunk guy flipped his lid. Everyone was watching him and I thought I'd go for it."

"But that man, Jonesy, he was sitting at the seat underneath. How did he not notice?" said Arnold.

"Easy, he was too busy watching them other two pull out half a torso from under the wheel. Strike while the iron is hot, eh?"

"They're going to go mental when they find out you've stolen it," said Arnold. "They'll probably kick you off the bus and feed you to those things."

"I'll be fine," said Connor leaning back in his seat once again. "We'll just say that guy must have took it."

"What guy?" said Benny.

"The guy who freaked out and ran out the back door. I heard he stole that stuff from above Jonesy's head while those other two were trying to fix the wheel. What an utter bastard, eh?"

"You're unbelievable," said Arnold shaking his head. "Okay, then. Next question. What is it?"

"Hang on, play cool."

"What you mean?" said Benny.

Connor nodded towards the front of bus where Tom was standing staring directly at the open locker.

"Be cool, be cool, it wasn't me, remember?" said Connor as they all watched Tom frantically look inside. "Or we could blame it on that fat guy who he threw out the window? Either way, it still wasn't me."

Tom turned to Frankie who simply shrugged his shoulders. He looked over to Jonesy who simply shook his head as he continued to drive. Clearly frustrated and confused, Tom sat back down.

"Looks like you're in the clear," said Benny. "So what was it then?"

Connor looked around to see if anyone was watching, before slipping a small plastic card to Benny. Benny glanced up to see if the three at the front were watching, then examined the card.

"Ryan Purcell, science team security level three," he read out quietly. Beside the writing there was a picture of a bearded man with large glasses on the card. He flipped it over, saw it was blank except for a metallic strip, then handed it over to Arnold.

"That's not all," said Connor. "This is even more interesting." He pulled out from under his jacket a small handheld tape player. He passed it to Benny.

"This looks old. I didn't think people still used these," he said as he examined it, while still keeping an eye on Tom at the front."

"This is some sort of Dictaphone," said Arnold as it was passed to him.

"Don't know," said Connor. "This is the first I really got a chance to look at it."

Arnold handed both the card and player over towards Connor, but he simply shook his head.

"It's okay, you keep them."

"What? You bastard!" snapped Arnold.

"You got bigger pockets than me. Besides, he probably trusts you more than me."

"I swear to God," muttered Arnold as he looked to Benny, unsure what to do with the stolen goods he just received. He then saw Tom standing up and turning once again to face the bus. Quickly he shoved the player and card into his pocket, where it chinked several times as it made contact with the pair of handcuffs he still had hidden.

"Ladies and gentlemen," Tom announced. "I am pleased to inform you all that we have arrived at our destination. Welcome to your new home."

Chapter 15

The bus reached the cast iron gates of a huge white building surrounded by a tall stone wall. Benny watched from the window as a young man in a white shirt and black tie, frantically opened the gates and waved the bus through. Soon as it passed he closed and locked them again.

The bus drove slowly along the short driveway up in front of the main building. A burly man wearing the now familiar white shirt and black tie stood at the bottom of the steps to the building and waved them down.

"Could the woman and children form a line here. The men form a line here," he shouted into a megaphone as he pointed to spots on the ground.

"What the hell is going on here," muttered Benny to Arnold, as they both disembarked the bus.

"God knows," he replied. "I don't like it already."

"Beats being out there with those things I guess," said Connor joining them.

A second bus drove up the drive way and then pulled up alongside theirs. It was much fuller than the bus they had been on.

"I said, could we have the men on this side, and the women and children over here, please!" shouted the man again. "We've a lot of people to get sorted tonight!"

Stacey was next off, followed by Beth who helped Maggie down the steps, then Laura holding Kerry and Eddie in each hand. The young couple who sat near the back of the bus stepped off as well.

"Right over here, ladies, please," shouted the man again, pointing to a stern looking middle aged woman wearing a skirt and shirt in the same black and white colour scheme as him.

"Mathew, I don't want to leave you," said the teenage girl holding on tight to her boyfriend as she began to cry.

"It's alright, Caroline," he said, trying his best to comfort her. "We're safe now."

"Your boyfriend is quite right, my dear girl," called Tom from inside the bus. "You have nothing to fear anymore. Now hurry along. We've a lot of people to house tonight."

Caroline looked at Mathew tearfully like a child on her first day of school. Mathew kissed her.

"Come on, lover boy," shouted Connor as he grabbed Mathew by the shoulder and pulled him over. "Let's not piss off our guests just yet."

Caroline stood there flabbergasted as she watched Mathew being taken over towards the three males. Stacey slowly approached her and nodded to her to join them.

Benny looked up at the imposing building in front of him, standing at least three storeys tall from what he could make out. It reminded him of the pictures he had seen in old history books and movies of plantations from the Deep South.

"You'll not be going in there yet, son", said Tom, seeing Benny taking an interest in it. "The men's dorms are over there."

He pointed to the left where there was a single story building thirty metres away. Benny turned around to see Beth, Stacey and Maggie's family disappear behind a line of other woman and children who were on the second bus.

"Okay, ladies," shouted Frankie, clearly addressing the dozen or so males of various ages who had lined up behind Benny and the others from the bus. "We're taking you to your quarters for the night. The big cheeses will address you all in the morning so save all your questions and bullshit for then. Okay?"

"Got to love these guys, eh?" whispered Connor to Arnold.

"Yeah, they've a certain charm to them," replied Arnold.

Frankie led the men towards the male dormitory. Benny looked behind him to see the woman and children being led off towards another dormitory on the other side of the grounds. Out of the corner of his eye, he saw Tom talking intently with the priest who was on the bus with them.

"What you think Tom and the priest are talking about?" he asked Arnold as they continued walking.

"Beats me," said Arnold as he quickly glanced over. "Lets just keep our heads down for a bit. Just until we know what these guys are up to."

"Where are we going," Stacey asked the stern looking woman as they were all led towards the female dorms.

"Questions will be answered later," she coldly answered. "Right now, it's important we get you all settled for the night."

"What about my boyfriend?" sniffled Caroline. "When will I see him again?"

"Tomorrow," snapped the woman. "Now come along, there's a lot of people to sort out."

The group was then taken inside were the woman then abruptly held her hand up.

"Stay here for a moment," she said before marching down the corridor.

"Reminds me of my old school," said Stacey, as she looked along the stark white walls.

"Didn't like there very much," said Beth, "Still think the jury's out on this place to be honest."

"Why can't we go back to Grannies house?" whined Kerry to her mother.

Just as Laura was about to tell her daughter to settle, the sound of heels clicking started to echo back along the hall and the stern woman marched back.

"You four are together?" she said waving to Laura, Maggie and the two children.

"Er, yes" said Laura nervously.

"We'll have you in this room," she said pointing towards the first door along the corridor. "Quickly, please. It's late now."

Laura glanced over towards Beth and gave a nervous smile.

"We'll see you all in the morning," said Beth trying her best to sound cheerful. "Meet you for breakfast, Kerry?"

"I said quickly," said the stern woman.

"See you in the morning," sighed Laura as she led her children and mother into the room allocated to them.

"Now then, you three." said the woman pointing to Beth,

Stacey and Caroline. "There's a room at the end I want you to fill. Follow me, girls."

The woman marched ahead as the three followed behind. As they walked further along the corridor they could hear shrieks and laughing coming from the room at the far end.

"What's going on down there?" demanded the woman, just as two peroxide blonde teenage girls, came racing out.

"Nothing," smirked one of them, as her friend did her best to suppress her laughing.

"Get back to your room and stay there," barked the woman, before turning to Beth and the others. "This will be yours. Hazel will be sharing with you."

Before they could ask who Hazel was, the woman strutted off. They went into the allocated room where four single beds greeted them. Sitting on the bed furthest away with her back to the room, was a large teenage goth girl. As the three entered the room she turned to look at them, showing her tear stained face, then quickly turned away.

"Are you Hazel?" asked Stacey cautiously as she slowly approached the girl. She sat down beside her.

"Yeah," replied Hazel sadly.

"Those two girls who were here, you know them?"

"Yeah," snarled Hazel, trying the best to hold back a flood of tears." The world goes to shit, people turn into monsters and kill each other, and yet those bitches are among the ones who get to live."

"I take it they're not friends of yours?" asked Stacey.

"God, no! They're just some stuck up bitches I have to see at school everyday. Now I get to see them here everyday."

"You stick with us," said Beth sitting down on the other side of Hazel. "They give you any more trouble they'll have us to deal with. Right, girls?"

"Right, Beth," said Stacey, putting her arm around Hazel. "You're with the cool group now, and we look out for each other."

Hazel looked up at Stacey and forced herself to smile.

"Thanks," she said softly. "Never been in the cool group before. Or a group."

"Me neither," said Beth, also putting her arm round Hazel.

"I guess I'm the same." said Caroline, sitting down on the bed opposite the others.

"Well you're all part of this group now, girls," said Stacey smiling with pride. "Stace and the cool cats."

"Huh?" said Hazel.

"So this is our room then?" said Connor as he walked into the four bed room. "What's the number for room service? I have a habit of getting hungry in the middle of the night."

"Just stay here until morning," came the gruff voice from the door. "And keep the noise down. There's a lot of people here and we don't want to hear you."

"It's alright," said Arnold. "We'll cause you no trouble."

"Good!" said Frankie as he pushed Benny, then Mathew into the room and then slammed the door.

"I really love the service here," said Connor as he lay down on one of the beds and stretched out. "Bed's not that comfy either. It'll not be getting a five star review from me."

"I hope Caroline's alright, said Mathew starting to pace around what little floor space there was in the small room. "She's probably worried sick. I should go find her or something."

"Just sit down and don't do anything stupid," said Arnold, putting his hands out to stop Mathew moving. "She'll be fine."

"Yeah, Matt," said Connor stretching out and putting his hands behind his head making himself more comfortable. "I would even bet that they've got a better place than we do. They probably have nice quilted toilet paper while we get sandpaper or a cheese grater."

"Er, It's Mathew," said Mathew.

"Yeah, I know," said Connor. "I heard you're girlfriend call you it. Put two and two together and reckoned it was probably your name."

"No, it's not that. You called me Matt. Caroline hates it when people shorten names. Especially mine."

"Oooooh, sorry," replied Connor mockingly. "Benjamin, would you pass on my sincere apologies to our young friend, Mathew here."

"Actually, my full name's Bernard," said Benny.

"Oh for Christ's sake," said Connor as he pulled the pillow out from beneath him and then placed it over his head. "Wake me when all this is over."

"Get that pillow off your face," said Arnold, as he dropped

something onto Connor's stomach.

"Shit! What's that?"

"That Dictaphone you stole and got me to stash," said Arnold. "Play it."

"You want me to play it now?" asked Connor as he pressed the eject button and removed the tape. He noticed on one side of the tape something scrawled in biro.

'Project 130K0R'

Benny slowly opened the door and peered out.

"It's clear," he whispered. "There's no one about."

"Right, everyone. Gather round," said Connor putting the tape back in the player and sitting up. "Everyone comfortable? Then we'll begin."

The group all huddled close as Connor pressed play.

Chapter 16

<Click>

Is this thing on?

Hello?

Hello.

Testing

Testing

One Two Three

Mary had a little lamb.

Right, not sure if this thing is working but here goes. My name is Ryan Purcell and I have been recently been transferred from department thirty-four D to department twelve B. I'm pretty excited as this is a top secret project. So if they knew I was making this recording I'd be up to my eyes in shit. So why do this? Why risk my job prospects? Why risk my very life?

Well I'll tell you.

I'm one mad crazy bastard. That's just me, not giving a damn. I might be a respected young scientist allowed into an inner secret circle within a secret area of government science research but at the same time, I'm a man who plays by his own rules and.......what?

No, mum!

Yes, I'll be down in a minute!

No, I'm not swearing!

No, I'm not doing...that!

Ohh for fu-

<Click>

I've had my first briefing. I'll be working with another guy called Sean O'Neill. Basically they told us nothing. Well next to nothing. Except on how everything is top secret and how if we divulge anything we're liable for prosecution and blah blah blah. God why do they even bother? Whatever they got me working on, it has to be something major. All I really know that I didn't know before was the project name.

Project One Three Zero Kay Zero Ar.

Catchy, huh? I'll probably just call it the Project, or just One Three. No way I'm sprouting that every time.

<Click>

Another boring day. Spent all day playing chess with Sean. He's pretty shit, but he takes losing quite well.

Wish they would get us doing something soon cause I'm absolutely wasted here doing nothing. Sean's talking about bringing in Hungry Hippos game. I don't know if he's taking the piss or not.

<Click>

Seems Sean wasn't joking.
I won the first game, but it wasn't until Sean said we should put money on it that he started winning.

Bastard.

I'm bringing in Guess Who tomorrow.

<Click>

Seems the fun and games are over. We're told that item One Three is due to arrive with us tomorrow. About time I say, cause I'm fed up with playing games with Sean. I'm convinced he's cheating, especially since he only wins when there's money involved.

Bastard.

I'm never playing Guess Who ever again. Stupid game anyway.

<Click>

Finally something happened today. Not much really. In the morning Sean wanted to see if I was up for winning back some of the money he took off me. I told him to piss off. He then produced Buckaroo. I'll admit I was tempted and would have taken his challenge if the special container hadn't arrived.

Unfortunately we were ushered out of the main lab while fifty soldiers came in, pointing their rifles at anything that moved. It was strange, as I always imagined soldiers to be big bad ass kicking bad asses, but there were quite a few of them who looked scared. Properly scared. I swear one of them looked like he was going to lose it completely.

It wasn't just the soldiers who were off. Some of the lab

supervisor looked really freaked out but they won't tell us why. How the hell are we supposed to do any research if they won't tell us what we're working with or what we're supposed to be doing.

For some reason, half the soldiers are remaining on site. I'm curious to know what exactly project One Three is.

First thing tomorrow, I'm kicking Sean's ass in Buckaroo.

<Click>

I hate Sean.

<Click>

Bastard.

<Click>

I still don't know why we're here. Sean thinks he's here just to take money from me. I'd love to punch him in his smug face. For the past couple of days we've been sitting outside the main lab while the more senior staff get to go in. I don't know what they're doing in there, but they got searched and scanned and God knows what else before being allowed in.

I still don't like the soldiers being here. Normally having soldiers guarding somewhere would fill you with confidence but for some reason they have me on edge. Maybe it's because some of them look like they're going to cry. Wish they'd tell us why they have us here. Still, if they're happy to pay us then I shouldn't complain, but I wish I was inside it a bit more. How's what I know now going to impress anyone?

<Click>

We're moving tomorrow. I was a bit peeved at first but luckily they told us project One Three is coming with us. Unfortunately, we'll have to become residential on the new base. Mum's already being annoying; trying to make sure I have enough of my medicine. She really freaked out when I told her I've no idea how long I'll be away for or even were the base is. I'll have to be careful bringing this Dictaphone with me though. If they find it, I could be in a bit of trouble.

<Click>

We arrived this morning to find them transporting project One Three onto an army truck. Finally got a look at it. Not a great look but a look none the less. It's a large metal cylinder which appears to have several portholes around it. I couldn't be sure but there was something inside. I didn't get to a good enough look cause one of the solders grabbed me by the face and shoved me away. Despite telling him that I was part of the science team, he wasn't having any of it. Strange the way me and Sean have been treated seems to be accepted by the supervisors. They say we'll be briefed in more detail when we get settled into the new lab. They did admit to us that they have kept us in the dark a little longer than they intended but all will become clear.

It seems this secret base is a mile underneath a forest. Nice scenery if we were allowed out to see it. Found out Sean's sharing a room with me. He better not snore.

<Click>

Finally, had a briefing with one of our head supervisors, Doctor Lavery. Or Doctor Bob as some of the guys call him behind his back. Seems civil enough but from what I've been told, don't get on the wrong side of him because his mood can change back and forth very quickly.

According to Doctor Bob, the reason we're told so very little is because all up the chain of command, they know very little also. What they do know is, is that item One Three has been passed onto them from another department. The strange thing is that they don't even know what the previous department was. In fact, they're not even told where that department even got it from.

But we finally got to see it and I can understand why everyone is so scared.

It's a creature, barley alive. I don't think it's a man. Well maybe it still is one, or maybe it used to be, I just don't know. I peered into the chamber to see this… thing, almost preserved in the liquid. It looks like a human but its taller and scrawny looking. Sean described it best by saying it looked like a skeleton with rotting meat wrapped around it.

The eyes freaked me out the most. There isn't any. Just two dark holes but you know its looking at you. And what doesn't help is when its badly disconnected jaw, moves ever so slightly when you look at it. Almost as if it's talking to you. I dread to think what something like that would say.

I feel we're a little closer within the circle now that they've told us what we're working with. A few of the other members of the team have been talking to us about it, and it really is a mystery what it is. Theories were all listed off were it could have come from. They ranged from it being a Nazi science experiment from the war, to an alien from a crashed space ship, to an ancient demon underneath a pyramid in Egypt, to a radiation mutation in somewhere like Chernobyl or some shit. One of the soldiers is convinced it's an old Haitian witch doctor that got in too deep with black magic. Sean reckons it's a creature from another dimension that has either found a way to enter our world and has been captured or the government has found a

way to travel inter dimensionally and has picked up
this…thing.

Normally, if somebody suggested stupid shit like that, then they
would get told to stop reading comics, get a slap around the
head and then laughed at. But nobody's laughing. Nobody.

<Click>

Things just kicked off to a new level of craziness. Well, if Sean
was telling the truth, but I have no reason to doubt him because
he looked terrified himself. According to Sean one of the
scientists this morning began to freak out. He was waving a
bible and shouting about God's punishment to mankind. Lavery
ordered two soldiers to restrain him and take him away to
another room, where a single gun shot was heard thirty seconds
later. I told Sean that he must have been mistaken, as they
wouldn't just execute someone because they were having a
seizure. Sean still looked worried, and eventually told me that
he could have sworn that the scientist's eyes were bleeding.

Not sure what to think. Could One Three have something to do
with it? Surely that thing is sedated and the container it's in is
secure?
I noticed Sean was holding quite tight to a bible, presumingly
the one the scientist was carrying. We've been told that the lab

work is postponed for today. Strange, I was so keen to get started with doing something, now I'm not so sure.

<Click>

Well I got another look at One Three. It doesn't get any easier looking at it, especially when I'm convinced it's looking back at me and plotting something. There are more soldiers in the complex with a few of them based permanently around it. I got sent out before I really got to do anything or help with whatever experiments they're planning to do.

Sean's refused to go anywhere near it, staying in his quarters reading the bible. He's talking about quitting. Not even asking for a transfer. He wants to go and work in some dirt hole fast food joint and flip shit burgers for minimum wage. I tried to talk some sense into him, but he wasn't having any of it. I told him he couldn't just walk out. We're in a secure secret base and know too much as it is. He snapped back and said we know nothing and we know enough. Whatever happened to the happy, carefree guy who played Guess Who and Buckaroo with me and took near two days wages from me?

Maybe I shouldn't be so hard on Sean. I didn't see the scientist ranting and raving before being carted away. And this thing. This One Three, whatever it is, does freak me out a little bit too. But I'm not running. This is something big, I know it. I can feel it.

<Click>

Got speaking to one of the soldiers today. Seems he and a few
of the other soldiers aren't not so keen on the good Doctor Bob.
He thinks the man is clearly keeping stuff to himself which is
annoying the other scientists he's supposed to be working with.
I told him that they should be lucky because me and Sean are at
the bottom of the list when it comes to being in the know. He
said the soldiers couldn't give two shits how he treats his work
colleagues, but it does annoy them that he seems to be the only
one in the whole complex who gets to leave whenever he
wants. That was news to me. Apparently Lavery leaves the base
roughly twice a week and is usually gone for a day or two. I
never really noticed because I always assumed he was working
away or in his private quarters. So where does he go to?

<Click>

Something's wrong with Sean. I don't know what, but I'm told
he's been taken care off. I don't know what that means, and I
don't think I should pry. All I know is that he's no longer in the
same room as me and is being kept somewhere else.

As for One Three, work has finally started. A sample had to be
taken from the creature which proved to be interesting. One

poor bastard had to open the top of the container and an even unluckier bastard had to quickly take a swab from the creature. I was the lowly bastard holding the Petri dish to catch the sample. Couldn't quite get a good view of how exactly it went as there was a dozen people surrounding the container, ready to drag the guy taking the sample away. I heard a bloody curling unholy scream and then the guys all scrambled to close the container. The man with the scalpel came charging at me and dropped the sample into the dish. Just as I closed the lid, I was nearly knocked off my feet as I was dragged towards the freezer. I think it was Lavery who grabbed it out of my hands before I really knew what happened. To be honest, once it was taken from me I lost interest in the dish and turned to look at the thing.

It was thrashing about and making the most terrified howling. I was memorised. I just couldn't take my eyes off it. Then it stopped dead, stared right back at me and pointed. Then it tapped the glass and I lost it. I totally lost it. I pissed myself. The others dragged me away and out of the lab before the piss had even reached my boots. Lavery told me to go back to my quarters and take the rest of the day off. I can't believe I pissed myself.

<Click>

People are going crazy now. One of the more senior scientists told me that when they went to do some work on the Petri dish, they found it was empty. No trace of the sample they took at all. What's even worrying is that I'm told this isn't the first time a sample as gone missing. God knows where it could have gone to but I'm glad they're not blaming me. Some of these people are very angry and for supposedly the greatest minds in the country they're not acting very rationally. Maybe Sean was right.

<Click>

It's still crazy here. Think people have being arguing all day and through the night. I'm not sure if anymore work has been done since we took the sample. Lavery seems to be nowhere to be found. Maybe he's had enough and using his special shore leave privileges and gotten the hell out of here. I'm really not sure what to do. Even the soldiers are arguing amongst themselves. What the hell have we gotten into? What the hell have I got myself into?

<Click>

It's completely fallen apart. Everything. Now the scientists are arguing with the soldiers and it's only a matter of time before somebody does something stupid. The guys in charge are doing the best they can, but at this rate, they're going to lose control of the entire base. I've been speaking to one of the soldiers and he reckons a full scale mutiny is going to occur. He reckons we

should be prepared for whatever happens, and get ready to act.
I'm not sure what he means. Does he know something more
than I do? Wouldn't be difficult to be honest because all I know
is for some reason, there's a big heap of shit and it's been
catapulted at light speed through the biggest wind turbine.

I've noticed there are no soldiers guarding the lab One Three in
anymore. I don't know if they've moved it or the soldiers have
refused to go near it. I wish it to be the former but I fear it's the
latter.

<Click>

Shit just got very very real. I don't know why I'm even still
recording this. I'm hoping this somehow will get back to my
parents or my friends or someone who even knows me and get
this out there.
The mutiny has begun and a few of us are deserting ship. I'm
currently in the back of this army truck and we're getting the
hell out of here. I have no idea what was going on but it's a
bloodbath back there. Literally.
I woke up this morning to hear gunfire and screaming. I got out
and tried to get to where it was coming from. I don't know why
I didn't run away from it all. I wish to Christ that I did, because
I'll never forget what I saw.
Bodies everywhere. Bloody and...ripped to pieces. Actually
torn apart. I'm not making this shit up. They were tearing each

other to pieces. I can't get the screams out of my head, it was horrific. I saw three of the guys who I helped opened the container, pin down a soldier and...

They...
…They...
…They...

I don't know how to describe it. It was like a scene from a horror film. I just had to run. I wasn't the only one. There were a few others who were freaking out as well. I followed them, not really knowing what the plan was.

I saw Sean standing there in the corridor. I was glad to see him at first but then I saw his eyes. They were totally red. I called his name but he just stared right at me and then pounced at me with his mouth open. I swear if one of the soldiers hadn't shot him in the head, then he would have taken a chunk out of my throat.

Everything's a bit of a blur. I was shocked that my friend had attacked me, and then I was shocked when he had his brains blown out of his head in front of me. I think somebody grabbed me by the arm and dragged me into one of these trucks. We're getting out of here, thank God. I just hope Project One Three Zero Kay Zero Ar stays there in that base. It's nothing but bad news and I wish I had never come here.

<Click>

Chapter 17

The four guys all looked at each other in silence for what seemed like an age.

"What does everyone think?" asked Benny.

There was another period of silence.

"I don't know," said Arnold eventually.

"This is some serious shit," said Connor, lying down on his bed. "As if things weren't serious already."

"We should give this tape to someone here," said Mathew. "They might be able to do something."

"Whoa whoa whoa!" said Connor sitting straight up and pointing to Mathew. "We can't just go about handing that over stuff we've just nicked."

"You mean stuff that you nicked?" said Arnold.

"Well it's got your prints on it too," said Connor throwing it over to Arnold. "Either way, we can't just hand it back."

"What was the name on the card?" asked Benny.

Arnold threw the Dictaphone back to Connor, hitting him right between the legs. He pulled the card out and read the name out. "Ryan Purcell. That's the guy on the tape, wasn't it?"

He handed it over to Benny.

"This must be for the lab he was working in," said Benny looking at it. "It would probably get you through restricted areas."

"That's if you can find the lab," said Mathew. "That man on the tape didn't say where it was, did he?"

Benny thought for a moment.

"Actually, I think I might know-"

"Knock it down in there!"

The shout came from behind the door. Benny quickly placed the card in his pocket while Connor hid the Dictaphone under the pillow.

"Sorry," said Arnold.

There was a snort from behind the door and then they heard the man turn around and walk off.

"We'll talk about this in the morning," whispered Arnold. "Let's just get some sleep now and we'll sort this shit out later."

"What shall I do with this?" asked Connor, pointing to his pillow.

"Dunno," replied Arnold, as he lay down on his bed and turned his back to him.

Benny and Mathew, looked at each other, then did the same.

"Rise and shine, ladies. It's morning!"

"What time is it?" asked Stacey groggily.

"Seven o'clock," said the woman as she came into the room, with a basket of clothes. She placed it down in the middle of the floor.

"What's this?" said Caroline, struggling to get up.

"A new clean set of clothes for you girls," she said. "Nothing in black and nothing for a Saturday night in the disco. So there's going to be two of you not happy."

"So nothing new then," said Hazel as she began to half heartedly rumble through the basket. "You haven't got anything in my size anyway."

"Haven't I? Oh, sorry. Hopefully we'll get some in your size later today."

"You've got a delivery coming or something?" asked Beth, having a look herself.

"Something like that," replied the woman. "The showers are opposite this room and you lucky ladies are first. There's a towel for each of you. Don't take longer than five minutes." She then left the room, closing the door firmly behind her.

"So what have we got then?" said Stacey. "You think the guys got much better?"

"Wakey, wakey, ladies! Time to get up!"

"Another five minutes, mum" shouted Connor.

"I'm getting pretty sick of you!" screamed Frankie as he grabbed Connor's duvet and threw it off.

"Take it easy," said Connor, rubbing his face. "What's the rush?"

"I'll tell you what the rush is," said Frankie pointing his finger at Connor. "You four are coming out with us this morning scavenging."

"What?" said all four of them.

"You heard me. Seems you four are the youngest and most able bodied men we've picked up so that means you're amongst the lucky ones who get to go back out there."

"Wait," shouted Mathew. "Where's Caroline? I need to see her."

"That your pretty lady, lad?" laughed Frankie.

"And the others," piped up Benny. "Beth and Stacey and Maggie's family. We need to see them."

"It's not up to me, said Frankie, holding his hands up. "You'll probably see them at breakfast, but we've got to be heading out soon after."

"You're serious," said Arnold, standing up to Frankie. "You're really going to send us out of here?"

"Calm down there, son," said Frankie squaring up to Arnold. "You'll be going with me and Jonesy in one of the buses, and once we're finished we come straight back here."

"What we going out for?" said Mathew.

"I told you, its scavenging. We get what we can. Food, clothes, supplies and with a bit of luck, some other survivors."

"So you're giving us guns?" said Connor. "Hasta la vista, baby."

"Christ, no, son," said Frankie shaking his head. "I wouldn't trust you with a toilet brush if it was up to me. You'll be given an axe each. Once you've been trained and you prove you can fire a gun without blowing your dicks off, then you'll get one."

"Bloody marvelous," sighed Connor.

"Glad you agree," said Frankie. "There's showers down the hall but I wouldn't bother if I was you. You're going to get dirty very quickly out there. Once you girls get your make up on, head to the mess hall in the main building for something to eat.

Maybe you'll be able to kiss your pretty girls goodbye."

Frankie gave a dirty laugh and then left the room.

"This is just like work," said Connor, once he was sure Frankie was out of earshot. "Wonder if I can call in sick and play some Xbox."

"Looks like we're going to run out of food now," laughed one of the peroxide teens to her friend who then burst laughing also.

Hazel sighed and turned to walk away in the opposite direction when Beth put her arm around her.

"Forget them," she said. "You're with us."

Stacey, Caroline, Beth with Hazel walked into the mess hall and walked towards a free table at the far end of the hall. As Stacey walked past she accidentally on purpose clipped her elbow against the first girl's head.

"Hey," she said.

"Hmm?" replied Stacey. "Oh sorry, I never noticed you there. Must happen to you quite a bit, does it?"

"What?"

Stacey leaned over, got right in her face and said with a huge grin, "People not noticing you."

The girl stared at her, mouth wide open.

"Well, that's certainly one way to get yourself noticed by the men," said Stacey, pushing her finger into the girl's mouth and then quickly pulling it out again.

"At least I'm not a big fat lesbian," the girl snapped as she pointed to Hazel.

"I'm not a lesbian," screamed Hazel as she stormed over to the girl. "I can't even stand the sight of my own twat, let alone anyone else's!"

"Come on, Hazel," said Beth, trying to guide her away from the girls. "Just forget them. They're not worth it."

"Doesn't matter if you're a lesbian or not," squeaked the second girl. "You're still a fat cow."

"At least my nose isn't bent!" yelled out Hazel, and before the girl could question her she was greeted with a punch to the face. The girl let out a whelp as she fell to the floor, blood pouring from her nose.

Stacey and Beth both took a hold of Hazel and quickly pulled her over towards the table which Caroline reserved.

"And people think I'm trouble," said Connor, as he walked into the hall, noticing several people nursing a girl with a bloody nose.

Benny quickly looked around the room. He saw the small group of people huddled over the injured girl and then he looked over and saw Beth and the others at the far side. Beth noticed him and waved him over.

"What's been going on," he asked her as he glanced over at the commotion on the other side of the hall.

"Never mind," she said. "Come on, just sit down."

Mathew and Caroline quickly embraced in a kiss as Connor and Arnold pulled up a chair each and sat down around the table.

"This is Hazel. She's in the same room as us," said Beth.

"Hi, Hazel," said Benny smiling briefly at her then turning back to Beth." They want us to go out on a run."

"A what?"

"A run. Scavenging they call it. They need guys to go out and find things like food and clothes."

"We may even pick up some nice ladies," said Connor smiling. "Not that there isn't nice ladies here. I'm Connor, by the way. Don't think we had a chance to get introduced."

"They can't send us out," said Caroline fretting, after she had finished sucking Mathew's face. "They just can't."

"No, it's just me and the guys. They didn't say about sending you or the girls out," said Mathew.

"But why?" said Caroline as her eyes began to water.

"Somebody has to, I guess" said Arnold. "There's quite a few people in this place and they need to be looked after."

"Yeah, how many people do you think are here?" said Benny looking around the hall.

"Not sure," said Beth. "Think we're amongst the first up."

"You certainly are."

Everyone turned around to see Tom standing behind them smiling.

"Morning, Tom," said Arnold. "I hear we're doing pick-ups."

"Yes, you are." said Tom patting Arnold on the side of the shoulder. "Thank you very much for doing this for us. We really appreciate it."

"Well, when we heard you needed us, we just had to volunteer," said Connor smiling. "Personally I'm looking forward to heading out there."

Tom sensed Connor's sarcasm and turned to face him.

"I know it seems like we're throwing you out in the fire and I'm sorry you feel that way. But look around at the people who are coming in to eat. Very few of the men are as young and as physically able as you four. You know each other and will work well together. We really need you to do this, to help everyone here. We lost a lot of strong men yesterday. More than we can afford if I'm honest. We need you."

"When do we leave then," asked Benny.

"No time like the present," said Tom. "The sooner we get the groups out the better. We got taken surprise last night when it turned dark."

"What's happening?" asked Beth. "What's causing all this?"

Tom took a deep breath, but before he could answer Jonesy appeared from behind and tapped him on the shoulder.

"Excuse me one moment," said Tom who turned to speak to Jonesy just out of earshot of the others. He returned ten seconds later. "I'm sorry I need to speak to Robert. Gentleman, if you follow Jonesy out to the bus, Frankie will join you there and you'll be ready."

"You already to go, boys?" shouted Jonesy.

"I'll speak to you all when you get back. Good luck," said Tom who then calmly walked out of the hall.

"Mathew, you can't leave me," sobbed Caroline holding tight. "I'll go with you, just don't leave me."

"No, stay here where it's safe," he replied softly. "I'll be fine. I promise."

"You be careful too, guys," said Beth giving Benny, then Arnold a hug. Stacey then hugged them both as well.

"We'll be back," said Arnold. "Look after Maggie and the others for us."

"We will," said Stacey, doing her best to hold back tears.

"No hugs for me, girls?" said Connor holding his arms out.

"You be careful too," said Beth simply.

"Fair enough," he replied as he put his hands back down. "Okay Jonesy, old boy. Let's get this field trip going."

Chapter 18

"This is going to be one long day," muttered Frankie as he saw Jonesy walking over towards the bus with the four following behind. "We've only got three of these axes so one of you is going to have to do without."

"Here, before you start crying," said Jonesy pulling out a bowie knife from his side and handed it to Mathew. "You're the smallest so an axe might be a bit much for you, son."

"Thank you," said Mathew, unsure if Jonesy was helping him or mocking him.

"And one for each of you big boys," said Frankie holding three firefighter axes. "Don't be losing these cause you won't be getting another."

"Thanks," they all said as they were all issued with one.

"Hold on a moment!" shouted a woman coming out of the main building. They all turned around to see it was the stern looking woman.

"You've come to give me and Jonesy a goodbye kiss then, Doris?" laughed Frankie.

"Definitely not," she said indignant. "Robert has told me to give this to you to try out."

She handed him a plastic bottle filled with a clear liquid. Frankie snatched it off her and looked at it closely.

"Don't be drinking it now," she warned.

"I'm not stupid," he snapped back. "Did he not test it with those things he-"

"Shut up, you idiot," she shouted, taking a side glance at the four teenagers. She lowered her voice but Benny who was the closest was still able to make her out. "He wants to see how it works out in the field."

"Whatever," said Frankie unimpressed. He gave the bottle one final look over, before tossing it over to Arnold. "You hold onto this for us. Don't be doing anything retarded like drinking it."

"Don't worry, I won't," he said, giving it the same look over Frankie did, before placing it in his inside pocket.

"Last chance for a kiss goodbye, Doris," laughed Frankie. "No? Suit yourself. Okay ladies, all aboard."

"This is going to be a long day," Benny whispered to Arnold as they got on the bus.

"I hope you ladies like the breakfast," said a cheerful young man with large curly blonde hair. He placed down a tray with several bowls of porridge onto the table. He stepped back and smiled at the girls. "My name's Gregory. I work in the kitchen and if you need anything or have dietary requirements then let me know. I've been told to make sure you are well looked after."

"You're scared I'm going to start hitting people or something," said Hazel with a hint of shame in her voice.

Gregory laughed nervously. "Um, like I said, if you need anything you'll find me in the kitchen. I'll probably be busy trying to feed everyone here but I've never too busy to help out. That okay, girls?"

"Yes, Gregory," said Beth. "Thank you."

"You're welcome," he replied as he smiled at everyone in the group before quickly scurrying back to the kitchen.

"I know I really shouldn't have hit Grace," said Hazel as she took a spoonful of porridge.

"Do her no harm," smiled Beth. "Might make her think twice before opening her mouth like that."

"No, I mean, I should have hit Annabel. She's the worst of two."

"That was some punch you hit her with," said Caroline impressed. "You do karate or boxing?"

"No," said Hazel. She looked over towards the table were the two girls were sitting. Grace was holding a bloody towel to her face, while Annabel looked towards Hazel with a look of concern and confusion. "I've wanted to do that for a very long time."

"I don't think they're going to be bothering you again," said Beth.

"Thanks, guys. For everything," said Hazel, smiling nervously before looking back down at her porridge.

"There's Beth!" shouted a little girl. It was Kerry.

Kerry ran up to Beth and gave her a big hug.

"Hi, Kerry. Did you sleep well."

"No, Granny kept snoring and Eddie kept farting."

"Kerry!" scolded her mother, "That's not what we talk about at the breakfast table." Maggie then appeared holding Eddie in her arms.

"Don't think Laura got too much sleep either," she said. "Hope the food is better than the beds.

"It's porridge," said Beth as she and the girls all shifted along the table to make room. "Or at least, it kind of tastes like it."

"I guess we can't complain really," said Laura. "Where are the boys that were with you? They haven't woken up yet?"

Caroline bit down on her lip and then turned away.

"They've been sent out on one of the buses to look for people," said Stacey.

"You're joking," said Laura.

"They just left here a few minutes ago," said Beth.

"I knew there was something not good about this place," said Maggie in a hushed tone. "No good will come from being here."

"I'll get Kerry and Eddie some breakfast," said Laura quickly. "Come on you two. You want some as well, mum?"

"No, I'm fine," said Maggie. "Maybe a cup of tea and a slice of toast. Make it two slices, actually."

"There's a guy called Gregory," said Beth. "Ask for him and he'll get you sorted."

They all waited until Laura had left before continuing the conversation.

"You know what this place is," asked Beth.

Maggie looked around to make sure nobody could hear.

"They're one of those sinister religious cult groups. And not the good kind either."

"You sure?" said Stacey anxiously. "I thought I overheard Connor last night saying it was just a retreat place."

"I'm very sure. Don't be getting confused this place with that nice religious retreat place just outside of town. Father Maurice is a wonderful man who helps people. Not like this place including that man Thomas Casson."

They all looked over and saw Tom at the entrance to the hall, greeting and smiling with people as they came in.

"Seems friendly enough," said Stacey. "You really think he's trouble?"

"I don't trust him. I know he helped us, but really this place had a bad reputation long before all this madness began."

"So what do we do?" said Caroline. "We can't leave here. Where else could we go to? And maybe it's not that bad. You know how rumours can spread. Maybe it's a good place after all."

"There's no toast, mum," said Laura returning. "They're bringing the tea over now but they don't have any milk."

"Just gets worse," murmured Maggie.

"So where exactly are we heading to or are we driving about randomly?" shouted Arnold up to Frankie at the far end of the bus.

"We have a set route and location assigned to us," said Frankie, leaning round. "We're doing the places nearby. Be glad you're not on Mickey's bus. They're the ones going really far out."

"Yeah," said Jonesy. "They might not be back until tomorrow."

"You mean there's another group who's going to be out all night?" said Arnold.

"That's right, son. They're the really big boys on that run. That's why they all get to have guns on that bus."

"So how come you get to have a shotgun and him driving gets a gun," said Connor.

"Shut up," said Frankie. "You're really annoying." Jonesy burst out laughing which caused Frankie to laugh too. Connor slid down in his seat and once Frankie had turned around to face the front of the bus, he flipped his middle digit at him.

"Pair of assholes," he said to Benny and Arnold who was sitting in the seat across from him. Mathew sat behind them. "Here, what's with the bottle?"

"Beats me," said Arnold as he pulled it out. He threw it over towards Connor, who took the lid of a sniffed the liquid.

"Don't be drinking it, whatever you do," he said as he put the top back on and threw it back to Arnold. "Smells like some sort of chemical or something. Definitely not water anyway."

"So what's the point of it," said Benny. "What did that woman say we should do with it?"

"Apart from not drink it, I don't think she told us anything," said Mathew.

"Something tells me these two chuckle brothers aren't going to tell us either," said Connor.

"Here, hang on a minute," said Arnold getting out of his seat. "This looks familiar."

"What does," said Benny.

"We were on this road yesterday. It leads to that town we were in."

"Aw, shit!" said Benny. "There were hundreds of them things there! Hey, Frankie, you're making a mistake."

"What you crying about, boy?" shouted Frankie.

"You got to turn back," said Arnold walking up to Frankie.

"We nearly died here yesterday."

"Just get your ass back in that seat," snarled Frankie who stood up and pointed the shotgun right at Arnold.

"Hey, hey. Calm down, I'm not doing anything," said Arnold raising his hands while still holding the axe in one hand. "I'm just saying you need to come back with more guys, and more guns. What we have just won't cut it."

"Let me tell you, lad," said Frankie, slowly lowering his gun. "We know a lot more than you do. You might have been caught with your pants round your ankles, but Tom and Robert have kept us good and straight here. They made sure we were ready for this. And you know what? We damn well are."

"You tell the little prick, Frankie," said Jonesy continuing to drive into the town.

"We're not messing here," said Benny, walking up also with his hands up. "You're making a mistake. There's too many of them here for just us."

"That's where you're wrong, son," snarled Frankie. "Thanks to a little device we know when there's too many. You hear all that beeping noise?"

"Erm, no," said Benny.

"Exactly," said Frankie with a big smile as he picked up a black device from the bus dashboard. It was the same one Tom used the night before. "That bleeping noise lets us know if there are loads of them bastards around. And since there it hasn't started beeping, it means we're alright."

"You haven't turned it on," said Jonesy.

"What?"

"It's not on," said Jonesy. "Here give us here, I know where the switch is."

"It is on, Jonesy."

"No, it's not Frankie, you dickhead. You need to hold this button down for two seconds."

"Seriously, you two," said Connor. "If that thing of yours can let us know if we're up to our neck in shit, then I think you should make sure it's working."

"There you go," said Jonesy. "It's on now."

The machine then started to beep. A lot.

Chapter 19

Beth, Stacey, Hazel, Caroline, Maggie, Laura, Kerry and Eddie all finished their breakfast and sat outside on the grass lawn in front of the main building.

"Such a lovely day," said Laura, as she watched Kerry and Eddie throw a ball back and forth to each other. "It's almost a pity."

"Never liked the warm weather," said Hazel. "Prefer it when it's cold. Easier to deal with."

"Be easier if you didn't wear so much black, dear," said Maggie with a smile. "Every try a nice white blouse?"

"Ah they you are," shouted Doris from the main building. "I hope you enjoyed your breakfast."

"Yes, thank you," said Beth quickly before any body attempted to complain.

"That's good. I hear there was an incident between yourselves and another young lady. Would that be correct?"

Doris looked over towards Hazel who looked down to the ground.

"There'll be no more trouble between them and us," said Beth firmly. "It's over, I promise."

"Just make sure it is," said Doris. "We can't have disorder in here as well, now can we?"

"Um, excuse me, what was your name again, mrs..?" asked Stacey.

"Doris, Just call me Doris."

"Yes, Doris then. Do you know what is going on? Why is this all happening?"

"I don't really know entirely," she replied. "Thomas and Robert are calling a meeting for all you new arrivals in an hour or so inside the house. Give you all a little briefing on what will be happening from now on."

"How long are we going to have to stay here until this is over," asked Caroline.

Doris took a deep breath.

"I'm sorry to say this, but things are not going to go back to the way they used to be. Not tomorrow, next week, next year or ever."

"But it can't be," said Caroline. "There must be people somewhere in the world who can stop this."

"My dear girl, this is not just happening in our small corner of the world. This is a world wide event."

"What?" said Stacey. "Everywhere?"

Maggie got up and went over to Kerry and Eddie. She moved them further away out of earshot.

"I'm afraid so," said Doris, once the children and Maggie were far enough away. "It caught nearly everyone in the whole world by surprise. For some reason, certain portions of the world's population underwent some sort of change. Then those that changed tried to butcher those that did not."

"The whole world?" said Caroline.

"It may have only started in the early hours of yesterday morning, but the stories that have come through are terrifying.

Not even the Vatican was safe from all this. Tom told me his Holiness was spared the turning but seven altar boys weren't and they…well, you know what these people are capable of. The stories of Buckingham Palace are worse. You just don't want to know about the corgis."

"The Americans," said Caroline. "They must have a plan to save us all."

"Don't count on it. The President was one of the turned and according to one of the reports, him and the first lady had to be shot. Seemed they had taken a fancy to the vice president. Wasn't much left of him either."

"How do you know all this?" said Beth suspiciously.

"What do you mean?" asked Doris, a little taken back with Beth's question.

"You said all this started yesterday, right?"

"That is correct."

"So how come you're hearing about this already? I mean, the radio's not working, and didn't Maggie say the television wasn't working either? Our phones won't get a signal and Benny said the landline was just playing that weird chant that was coming out of the radio. How do you know what's being happening in Rome, Washington DC and Buckingham Palace?" Beth then realised she probably had gotten a little carried away and looked up at Doris, almost apologetically for her tone.

"Sorry, I shouldn't," she said.

"No, you're quite right, dear," said Doris surprisingly understandingly. "The truth is, I was told by Tom who was told by Robert. How he knows, I've no idea. You do bring up a very good point."

"Who's Robert," said Stacey. "We've met Tom but I still not sure on who he is."

"Tom Casson owns this sanctuary that protects us all," said Doris. "You owe him a great deal of thanks that he has opened the doors here and taken anyone in who needed it."

"Maggie was saying this was some sort of religious cult place," said Stacey, who promptly received a nudge from Laura.

"Some intolerant people may say that," said Doris proudly. "But this was a different type of sanctuary for many people who may have felt lost in life. A place where they can get together with similar souls and hear the good word."

"God, I ended up in the right place," grumbled Hazel. "At least I didn't have to hand over everything I owned to get in."

"And who's Robert?" asked Beth.

"Who's Robert indeed," said Doris slowly. "That is a question I really can't answer fully."

"You have met him?" asked Stacey.

"Yes, I have. Briefly though. He only arrived here about a week ago. Maybe less. It can be hard to keep track of days sometimes."

"So why did he come here?" asked Beth.

"I don't know, but when he arrived he spent a lot of time with Tom. I hardly saw Tom but they seemed to be talking and planning something together. It was the next couple of days when these other people arrived."

"Others?" said Laura.

"Those men who drive the buses. The ones with the guns."

"Ah yes," said Beth. "They did seem a little out of place."

"Yes, I must say I wasn't too happy with them being here either. Nor were most of the other residents here. Swearing and blaspheming just to get a rise out of us good folk. I really thought Tom must have lost his mind getting involved with them."

"So what happened when all this began to happen?" asked Beth. "These guys kept things from getting out of control?"

"Only very slightly," sighed Doris. "A huge number of people here turned. Including a few of the undesirables. Fortunately, the ones that didn't turn made sure the rest of us were safe and then they took care of, well, the ones that needed to be taken care of."

"So it was good they arrived then?" said Stacey.

"I suppose it was. A couple of times I really thought it was the end for all of us but thankfully we pulled through. Although I do question how reliable some of these men are. The two that went off with your friends forgot to lift their walkie talkie amongst other things. Thank goodness they're the ones not going too far but still, I think Tom or Robert plans to give them a wrap over the knuckles."

"You mean there's no way Benny and Arnold and the others can be contacted?" said Beth.

"Not until they come back, no." said Doris.

"Oh God," gasped Caroline. "We've no idea if they're…"

"They will be fine," said Doris cutting her off before she became too hysterical. "I told you, they're not going as far as the others and will probably be back later this afternoon. Please don't worry."

"Why are you sending people out," asked Caroline, slightly panicked. "It's dangerous, why can't we all just stay here?"

"The supplies here won't last forever. We also did lose a lot of good people, and I think that's why they want to pick up as many survivors as they can.

"They want us to live here and rebuild the world then?" said Caroline. "Just carry on as normal or what?"

"Easy, Caroline," said Beth.

"I don't know," said Doris sharply. "You will need hear what Tom has to say. He knows what's needed to be done. Now if you will excuse me, I still have work to do. I'll let you know when Tom is ready." She then returned to the main building.

"What you reckon, Beth," asked Stacey.

"I don't like it. I'm not totally sure on Tom and I really don't like the sound of this Robert, whoever he is. I just don't like it at all."

Chapter 20

"Get this bus in reverse now!" yelled Connor.

"That's what I'm doing!" shouted back Jonesy.

"Jesus, there's even more of them it seems," said Benny looking out the window. Red eyes had begun stumbling out from alleyways and side streets and onto the main road where the bus had stopped.

"At least they're not running at us anymore," said Mathew.

Jonesy reversed the bus back along the street, as several hundred red eyes began following it.

"Is it just me or are those dumb bastards even slower than before," said Frankie, looking out the front driver window. "Look at them."

Arnold and Benny joined Frankie at the front of the bus and looked out.

"Yeah, you're right," said Arnold.

"Maybe they tired themselves out from last night," said Benny.

"I reckon we shouldn't be so quick to run away, eh, boys?" laughed Frankie. "Open the door, Jonesy. Lets go for a little jog."

"Wait," said Benny. "That's just being stupid. There's still, what, a couple of hundred of them. They're still dangerous."

"You not scared are you, kid," said Frankie getting in Benny's face.

"No, it's just…"

"Good. Then you and me are first up. Open the door."

"The kid's right, Frankie," said Jonesy. "Let's not piss these things off if we don't have too."

"Now don't you be getting all queer on me now too, Jonesy." said Frankie raising his voice. He leaned over and pushed the button to open the door. "After you, lad."

"You're joking, right," shouted Benny.

"Of course, I am," laughed Frankie as he leaned over again and closed the door. "You should have seen your face. You looked like you were going to shit yourself."

"Yeah, real funny, Frankie," said Benny as he returned back to his seat.

"So we head back to base then?" said Arnold.

"Course not," said Frankie. "Robert would have a fit if we came back empty handed. Tom not so much, but that Rob guy, you don't want to piss him off."

"So what's the plan then?" said Arnold.

"Let me think," replied Frankie. "I reckon we could easily go in there on foot. Run through them all, raid a few shops and bring the loot on out."

"I say that's too dangerous," said Arnold. "They're slow alright and its easy to take out a few of them, but there's a lot of them. The numbers will beat us in the end."

"Well, we have a distraction then. We have Jonesy here in the bus, revving it up, blowing his horn and keeping these bastards' attention, while we grab what we can."

"This really the best plan you can think of," called Connor from the back. "In fact, you know what? I'm not even going to bother arguing with you about it."

"I'm warning you, son…" shouted Frankie.

"Okay, okay, let's get some sort of plan going at least," said Arnold trying to calm the situation. "How about this? Jonesy takes the bus back out of town, we jump out, then drives back in, while we follow way behind on foot, staying out of sight. While those things are all distracted, we see what we can get, if anything."

"Good God," muttered Mathew to Benny. "Your friend's almost as mad as they are."

"That's exactly my idea, son," said Frankie blatantly lying. "Of course, you forgot about the bit where we have the doors underneath the bus already open so we can just throw the shit in. But apart from that, you almost read my mind."

Frankie then gave Arnold's face a few slight slaps before turning to Jonesy and whispering to him.

"So what's the deal with this bottle then," said Arnold, pulling it out of his pocket and holding it up.

"Oh that," said Frankie, putting the shotgun down and taking the bottle out of Arnold's hand. "Hold your axe out and I'll show you."

Arnold looked at Frankie confused but went back to his seat and lifted his axe. He brought it up to Frankie and held the axe head out to him. With a smile, Frankie twisted the cap of the bottle and poured some of the liquid over the axe.

"What are you doing?"

"Here, take this," said Frankie handing the bottle to Arnold, while snatching the axe from his other hand. He then looked out the side window. "There's one there that's not going to cause too much hassle. Jonesy, open the door."

"This another one of your jokes," shouted Benny.

"No joke. Come out and join me and see for yourself."

"Just be quick, Frankie. There's still a few of them getting close," shouted Jonesy, as brought the bus to a stop and opened the door.

Frankie stepped out and took sight of the closest red eye stumbling towards him. It was a young woman, barely in her twenties dressed in a nurses uniform. He smiled to himself as he watched her slowly move towards him.

"You watching, boys?" he said as she got to within a few feet of him. He then held the axe head up against her face. The flesh on her face began to sizzle, as steam began to rise from her face. The red eye growled as Frankie pressed the flat part of the axe harder into the side of her face.

"What is that stuff?" said Benny as he watched from the bus window. "Some sort of acid?"

"If it was acid, wouldn't it burn through the bottle?" asked Mathew.

"Whatever it is, it's done a number on that girl's face," said Connor.

Frankie removed the axe from the red eyes face and took a step back to examine the damage. The whole side of the face was a drooping mess as it continued to burn and smother.

"Aw, she's not so pretty now," jeered Frankie as he took a swing of the axe, lobbing her head with one clean sweep. He gave the head a massive kick, clearing it down the road before jumping back on the bus. He handed the axe back to Arnold and picked up his shotgun. "I'd still rather have me old shotgun over that any day."

"What is this stuff," asked Arnold looking even more closely to the bottle.

"Beats me," said Frankie.

"That's some magic shit," said Jonesy, continuing to reverse the bus. "You going to radio back and tell them it works?"

"No need. They already know it works. I was there when they tested it this morning."

"You've been out already today?" said Benny. "Where did you go?"

"Er, nowhere. Mind your own business, kid."

Benny and Arnold both glanced at each, wondering why Frankie had become so cagey over the question.

"Right, this is where you fellas jump out," said Frankie once Jonesy had reversed the bus a good distance away from the town centre.

"You not coming with us?" asked Arnold.

"Somebody has to stay here and cover Jonesy. He can't drive and shoot at the same time, now can he?"

"That's so good of you volunteering to do that," said Connor. "Whatever would we all do without you."

"Just so you guys are all clear on the plan," said Frankie ignoring Connor. "There's a bag in the bit below the bus. You fill that up with what you can get. Me and Jonesy will circle back in about fifteen minutes and when we do, you throw it in and get aboard."

"Simple," said Connor sarcastically.

"Good."

The four of them got of the bus, all of them holding their axes except Mathew who was clutched his knife. Arnold opened the bottom compartment where a large travel bag lay. He grabbed it and slung it over his shoulder.

"There looked like there was a shop at the first corner," shouted Frankie from the bus door. "Get as many cans and shit as you can, and don't forget to get some smokes too. We're running low."

Frankie's head popped back inside and the door closed. The bus drove up ahead, horn blaring and grabbing the attention of the red eyes as it disappeared along the road.

"Fifteen minutes then?" said Benny. "We better get moving."

The road up into the town was surprisingly virtually clear of any red eyes. Occasionally there was a lone one, snatching and gawking, but they were easily avoided as the four of them dashed by.

"Looks like the plan is working," said Arnold to the others as they took cover behind an abandoned car at the side of the road. "That must be the shop there he was talking about."

Benny peered his head round and looked towards the small store. There was a clear route right to the shop door which he knew they could reach in seconds.

"Yeah, think you're right," he said. "You still got the bag, Arn?"

"Right here. Let's go!"

They all ran as fast as they could towards the door with Benny reaching it first. He pushed it, and like the charity shop yesterday, it was unlocked. They all dived through and Benny quickly shut it behind him.

"We did it," he exclaimed. "They didn't see us."

"We're getting good at this," said Arnold, removing the bag from his shoulder and unzipping it in the middle of the shop floor. "Now let's fill this up. Mathew, you hold one end and I'll hold the other."

"I'll make sure we're clear," said Benny dashing down to the back of the shop. "Yes, we're all clear."

With both of them holding the bag, Mathew and Arnold ran along the isles at the back of the shop, knocking as many cans and food packets as they could. Connor had jumped over the counter and began filling his pockets with packets of cigarettes and tobacco.

"What you bothering with that for," shouted Benny when we saw what he was doing.

"Don't worry, it's all personal use. I'm not giving any to the fathead brothers. You want some scratch cards while I'm here?"

"Shit, this is full already," shouted Arnold. "And it's heavy."

"Just as well," said Benny looking through the window. "Our bus is coming back now."

"That's not fifteen minutes," said Connor. "Not that I'm complaining."

"You guys get the bag, I'll get the door," said Benny with his hand on the door handle.

"Dammit," yelled Arnold, throwing down his axe and holding his side of the bag with both hands. Connor raced over, dropping his axe also and pushed Mathew aside. He then grabbed with both hands the other side of the bag.

Benny quickly opened the door but standing in the door way was a red eye. A tall average build middle aged man with a blatant comb over.

"Benny, watch out," shouted Connor, as Benny raised the axe handle up to pin the red eye's chest up against the door frame.

"Yeah, I see him!" shouted Benny, holding the axe tight as the red eye snapped his teeth towards him. "Mathew! You still got your knife?"

"Y-yes," stammered Mathew, as he reluctantly walked over, holding the knife in his shaking hands.

"Stab him in the head!" shouted Benny, pushing the axe harder against the red eye's body.

"You mean now?"

"Yes, now!" yelled back Benny.

"Um.."

"Jesus, Matt," shouted Connor. "Did you leave your balls in girlfriend's handbag? Just stab it!"

Mathew looked over at Connor then back to the red eye. He gritted his teeth and thrust the knife at the red eye's throat. It pierced it and the knife pushed into the flesh by about two inches. Mathew let go of the knife as it dangled from the red eye's throat. Benny took a step back, releasing the hold he had with the axe. He then grabbed the knife handle and pushed it further into the throat. The force of it caused the red eye to lose its balance and fall to the floor gargling and spluttering as blood flowed from its mouth.

"You did good," said Benny trying to reassure Mathew.

"Let's just go," shouted Arnold shoving past while still carrying the bag with Connor.

Benny placed his foot on the red eye's head and then pulled the knife out. He wiped it on the trouser leg of the red eye before handing it back to Mathew.

"Come on, we better get this bus."

They both ran outside following after the other two.

"Over here!" shouted Arnold, dropping the bag. He began waving frantically at the bus which was being followed a herd of red eyes. The bus approached them and slowed down to a stop.

"Get the bag in!" shouted Frankie from the window. "Hurry!"

Benny opened the compartment and helped Arnold and Connor load it inside. Once in, he slammed the door shut.

"Quick, open up," shouted Mathew, knocking on the bus door.

"Can't do that, boys," shouted Frankie from the window.

"What?" yelled all four of them.

Frankie never replied but pointed a handgun out the window instead. He aimed it at Arnold.

"What the hell you doing?" he shouted.

Frankie fired just as Arnold tried to dive out of the way. He landed on the ground but then he realised that his side was becoming very wet as felt liquid beginning to pour down.

"You bastards!" he screamed as he saw the bus drive off leaving them all behind.

Chapter 21

"So what crap are we going to be told now," said Hazel, as they were all brought back into the canteen.

"I don't know," said Beth. "I just got a bad feeling about this place."

They all sat around the same table they were at for breakfast and watched the other residents enter.

Annabel and Grace were the first to walk in and once they both spotted Hazel they went straight to the furthest table away from them. Behind them walked in fifteen women, most of them middle aged, with a few in their mid-twenties and a few elderly. All of them nervously took seats and sat down in silence.

Several few seconds later Doris entered the hall with nine men walking behind her. Like the woman, they nervously took their seats. A few of them looked round and gave polite nods to the others, trying their best to mask any concerns and fears that they had.

"Is that everyone here then?" asked Tom who walked confidently into the room. "Good to see you all here."

Tom made his way to the top end of the hall, where a small platform awaited him. He turned to address the room.

"People, first let me tell you, you are finally safe and welcome."

Doris started to clap, which the people in the room reluctantly began to join in.

"Thank you, thank you," said Tom with a huge smile on his face.

"Asshole," Hazel whispered to Beth as she unenthusiastically clapped.

"I know you've probably just experienced the worst day of your lives yesterday but today will be the first day of the best days of your life."

"Total asshole," Hazel whispered again. Beth nodded slightly in agreement.

"Some of you may think you have just survived, well you haven't. You have more than survived. You have been chosen."

"Chosen for what?" shouted out an elderly man, clearly not in awe but immediately regretting it once he realised the whole room was looking at him.

"We are alive for a reason," said Tom looking at the man.

"Many people on this world were chosen but in a different way than we were. They were chosen to be removed from the new world that we will inherit."

"Okay, this is starting to freak even me out a bit," gulped Hazel.

"My friends, this is the Flood for our times and this is our Ark. As we speak, we have several groups heading out onto the waters and bringing in other good people who have been chosen. Soon the madness will end and left behind there will be us who will inherit this paradise resculptured for us."

"This is madness!" shouted Maggie. "I don't know what Bible you read and believe, but it's not the one I do. I know many good people who aren't here, and I won't have you say they weren't good enough to be saved!"

"Mother, please," pleaded Laura, trying to calm her mother down.

"It's quite alright," replied Tom. "I understand many of us still need time to readjust to the world now. It is a lot to take in, but you must believe me when I tell you, you have nothing to fear or worry any more. You are home."

"I see you're doing a fine job settling everyone in, Tom." Everyone turned around to see who the deep booming voice belonged to. A tall man, appearing to be in his early forties, dressed in an entirely black suit, strolled to the front of the hall up to Tom.

"Robert," Tom greeted him nervously. "Thank you for joining us. Ladies and gentlemen, may I introduce to you, Robert Lavery."

Robert modestly smiled and held his hand up to halt an applause that he was expecting.

"Please, everyone. The important thing for everyone is to remain completely calm and follow our instructions. Things are still not entirely over yet. There is much work for everyone to do, but if you listen and do as you're told, you will be safe."

"Two assholes now," whispered Hazel again.

"First of all, I want to thank Tom here," said Robert, pointing to Tom. "Tom has provided us with a safe place to live and for important work to be done to ensure our safety. So please, give this man, and the people he was working for him, a warm round of applause."

Reluctantly everyone in the room gave a mandatory couple of claps as they looked around to each other.

"Good," said Robert pleased with himself. "I would love to talk to you all individually right now, and I know I will throughout the natural course of the days to come, but as you can imagine I am currently extremely busy with many things. However, Tom and his staff will do everything in their abilities to make everything as comfortable as reasonably possible. You will find the main house has many facilities for you to make the most of. There is a library on the first floor as well as a fairly modest workout room for those who wish to keep themselves in shape. There's also a few empty rooms for those who want some quiet reflection time. After what some of you may have experienced it could do you the world of good."

"Didn't say there was a bar here," whispered Hazel. "I think I would rather get wasted." She looked up and saw Robert staring back at her.

"Oh shit," she said under her breath. Robert took several steps towards her.

"I do believe Tom has a music room here as well," he said still looking at Hazel. "There's a piano and I do believe there's a few guitars there if I'm not mistaken. Is that right, Tom"

"Er, yes, Robert there is," said Tom, taken by surprise. "I know there's three acoustic ones and I even think we've an electric one as well."

"Ah," said Robert still looking at Hazel with an unnerving smile. "You hear that? Perhaps you could play some of that pop music which I can tell you must like so much."

"Yeah, I could," said Hazel quietly as she glanced over to Beth.

"The weather is lovely outside, people" said Robert addressing the rest of the crowd. "If you wish to go outside and make the most of it, then please do. If you wish to return to the dormitories then you are free to do so also. And if you wish to use the facilities then just ask and the staff here shall show you the way. I would ask only if you keep yourself just to the bottom two floors of this building. Like I said, we have important work going on the floors above which will benefit us all, and I wouldn't want any of it to be disturbed."

"Wonder what sort of work that could be," said Beth to Stacey, making sure she said it quieter than Hazel did.

"Yes, thank you, Robert," said Tom, now standing forward to address the crowd. "Please, make yourselves at home. This after all, is now your home."

Slowly the crowd began to make their way out of the canteen, everyone not quite sure where they should be going but felt obliged to leave and make the most of Robert's suggestions.

"Could I just speak to you four ladies, please?" called Robert.

"Um, you mean us?" said Beth turning around.

"Yes, you four," said Robert pointing to Stacey then to Hazel then to Caroline. "Could I just speak to you in private for a moment."

"What do you want to speak to them about," said Maggie abruptly.

"Mum!" exclaimed Laura.

"You've nothing to worry about, madam," said Robert once again with the uneasy smile. "It's only for a moment and they will be back down with you shortly. Why don't you and your daughter take the children out to the back yard and play some games?"

"It's okay, Maggie," said Beth. "You take Kerry and Eddie out and we'll all join you for a game or two once we've spoken to Robert. Won't you like that, Kerry?"

Maggie looked over to Robert and gave him a cold stare. Laura put her arm around her mother and gently guided her out of the room, while Maggie continued with the gaze.

"She means well," said Beth apologetically.

"That I have no doubt," said Robert. "Now come with me ladies. There's a lift at the back here."

"A lift?" said Stacey as they followed Robert out of the room, down a narrow corridor and to the lift doors. "Where is it we're going?"

"The top floor. It's my personal quarters up there."

"Didn't you say we weren't allowed up there," said Hazel. "What was it, just the bottom two floors?"

Robert laughed to himself. "I think you'll be safe enough with me. Just don't go wondering off on your own when you're up here."

"Why's that?" said Caroline starting to get worried. "What's up there?"

"Don't worry, I'm joking," said Robert. "You're very safe here. Now after you ladies."

The four girls and Robert entered the small lift and took it all the way up to the top floor.

"We could have walked it," said Robert as the lift rattled as it climbed up. "But let's not make life difficult for ourselves when we don't have to. Would you agree, ladies?"

"I guess," said Beth.

When they reached the top, Robert left the lift first and walked down the top floor corridor.

"This way, please," he called to them as he stopped outside one of the doors. "This is my own personal quarters. Please excuse any mess."

"So how come you get a room to yourself then?" said Hazel as Robert opened the doors to his room and walked in. "Or do you have to share with the flatmate from hell?"

The girls followed him in. It was an extremely grand room that looked just like a picture from the brochure of a posh London hotel. Even the air itself had a smell and taste that for a brief moment made them all forget that the world was falling apart.

"This bathroom's bigger than my room," said Stacey as she popped her head round the bathroom door to her side. Inside the marble room, was a huge bath big enough for several people. Stacy quickly left the room and closed the door, feeling unsure of what to make of the oversized bath.

"There's another two rooms across the hall that are unoccupied," said Robert as he leaned up against the four poster bed. "I think you ladies will find them quite comfortable. Unfortunately I can't offer you a room each as much as I would like."

"This is all very kind of you, Robert, and we are grateful," said Beth. "But I couldn't stay up here when I knew Maggie and her family were living in such basic housing down below."

"I can understand that and respect that, but believe me, we're working on upgrading the accommodation. Things will improve for them greatly."

"Why not move the four of them up here," said Beth. "They've two young kids, surely it would make more sense to move them up here."

"Why us," said Caroline. "Don't get me wrong, I appreciate it very much, but I wouldn't feel right if Connor and the others were staying so far away."

Robert sighed and looked down to the ground. "I have some bad news for you. I thought I might soften the blow a bit by offering you to come live up here."

"Bad news?" asked Beth.

"Yes, you might want to sit down. All of you."

"What is it?" said Stacey.

"The young men who you arrived with."

"What about them?" said Beth beginning to get worried.

"We received a message from Frankie not so long ago."

"A message? From, like, a walkie talkie?" said Beth, trying to keep her cool. She glanced across to the other girls before looking back to Robert.

"Yes, it was a message came through from Frank's convoy. I'm afraid it's not good news" said Robert, not taking his eyes of the floor.

"Beth glanced again very slightly to the other girls in the room before walking closer to Robert.

"What did he say?"

"They were attacked. They didn't make it. I'm sorry."

"What you mean, they didn't make it?" said Caroline raising her voice.

"They're dead," said Robert looking up with a pitiful expression. "Frank and Jones were able to get away, but the others didn't."

Caroline held her hand up to her mouth and then turned away.

"I think I'm going to be sick."

Beth quickly put her arm around her and pushed her into the bathroom. From there Stacey, Hazel and Robert heard the sounds of retching and sobbing.

"I'll leave you ladies in peace to come to terms with what's just happened," said Robert getting up and moving towards the door. "Whenever you're ready, come down to the bottom floor and we'll discuss moving you up here. It's the least I can do considering what you've just been through."

"Thank you," said Stacey timidity. "We'll be down shortly."

"Take your time," said Robert as he gave a brief smile before leaving the room.

Stacey and Hazel both looked at each other in silence for a few seconds, giving time for Robert to be completely clear of the door.

"What do you think?" said Stacey.

"I smell bullshit," said Hazel. "What was it Doris told us? They left behind their walkie talkie?"

"Yeah, that's what I thought too. So somebody's lying to us and I don't think it's Doris."

"So why tell us he got a message from them when we he couldn't have?"

The bathroom door opened and Beth and Caroline came out.

"I'm okay," said Caroline, wiping her teary eyes. "Just didn't feel so good there."

"You know he's lying," Hazel said to her. "We know he's full of shit."

"I know," said Caroline softly. "It just when he said it, I just realised I'd be lost without Mathew."

"So what do we do now?" said Stacy looking to Beth.

Beth thought for a moment.

"We need to get out of here. Get Maggie and her family and go find the guys."

"Then what?" said Stacey. "If we leave we can't come back here, so where do we go to?"

"I don't like it here," said Hazel. "This can't be the only safe place to be. There's got to be other places like this."

"Yes, there has to be," said Beth. "Somewhere more proper than this place anyway. I refuse to believe these are the only people prepared for this."

"So it's settled," said Hazel. "We're getting the hell out of here and not coming back."

"But when and how?" said Stacey. "Do we just walk out of here? And how are we even going to find Arnold and Benny? Where do we even start?"

"I'm not sure," said Beth. "But we'll think of something. We have to."

Chapter 22

"Arnold!" shouted Benny running over.

"He got me," wheezed Arnold lying on the ground, "He got me."

"Let me see," said Mathew kneeling down closer to Arnold.

"Guys," said Connor as he looked over his shoulder. "We need to move him damn quick cause those things are about literally twenty seconds from reaching us."

"Benny, just put pressure on the wound," said Mathew.

"Where?" asked Benny.

"Just here, where the…hang on a minute."

"What is it?" asked Arnold.

"Arnold, you're not shot."

"What?" said Arnold sitting up.

"This is water."

Arnold looked down and touched his chest where he had felt what he thought was blood. There was a hole in his jacket were a bullet had gone through. He quickly stood up and put his hand in his pocket which had the bullet hole. He pulled out the now empty plastic bottle which had a hole in it and the remains of a bullet inside.

"Shit," said Arnold embarrassed, as he threw the bottle away.

"How did that happen," said Mathew baffled.

Arnold felt something else in his pocket that had become wet. He reached in to pull it out, forgetting completely what he had in there. Once he pulled it out he realised he probably shouldn't have.

"Handcuffs?" said Mathew. "Why have you got handcuffs? You a cop or something?"

"They're not mine," said Arnold quickly throwing them to the ground.

"The bullet must have hit the metal," said Benny picking them up and looking at them closely. "You lucky bastard, Arn. Where did these come from?"

"Er, found them ages ago. Keep them if you want."

"Let's just go now," shouted Connor putting his arms out to shepherd the group forward. The rest of them looked back to see the nearest red eye was only a few feet away and looking hungry.

"Where are we going?" said Mathew as they ran up the street, leading out of the town.

"Just keep going," shouted Arnold back. He looked over to make sure everyone else was following behind.

"I think we're fine," said Benny slowing down his speed to a brisk jog. "They're slow. Really slow. Let's not kill ourselves."

"He's right," said Connor slowing down to match Benny's speed. "We need to think about what we're doing."

"Well what should we be doing?" said Mathew also slowing down.

"We need to get back and get the girls," said Benny. "They're not safe there."

"Yeah, what the hell are those bastards playing at," said Connor. "They're definitely not getting any smokes now."

"I didn't trust those guys," said Mathew. "I just didn't expect them to leave us here to die."

"We're not dead yet," shouted Arnold. "We can't give up. We'll find a way."

"I've still got my axe," said Benny. "Mathew, you still got your knife?"

"Yeah," said Mathew. "That all the weapons we got?"

"Afraid so," said Arnold. "Me and Connor both dropped ours carrying that bag, which them two scum bags got as well."

They carried on along the road, easily outpacing the red eyes following behind them until they reached the outskirts.

"We can't walk the whole way back," said Mathew. "It will be too late."

"We could reach Maggie's house easy enough," said Benny. "If we could find the key we could take my dads car."

"You remember where you dropped it?" said Arnold.

"I've no idea," said Benny "Things were a bit crazy last night."

"They still are," said Connor.

"We'll have to try," said Arnold. "I gave you them in the attic so we'll start there and trace your steps. Your dad's car is the only way to get back to the girls in time."

"What way then?" said Mathew.

"This direction," said Arnold taking the lead. "We should reach it in an hour at the most."

Chapter 23

Beth and the rest of the girls along with Maggie and her family sat in the canteen along with all the other survivors.

"This only reinforces my belief that this place and these people are dangerous," whispered Maggie, after Beth explained what had happened earlier. "I agree, we should leave and go back to my place. We can stay there and wait until the proper help arrives."

"Proper help, mum?" asked Laura, unsure of her mother's suggestion. "This is the only people that have come along. These people could keep us safe."

"We can keep ourselves safe," her mother said back. "My house is big enough to hold us all. We might not have a big wall around us like place does, but we can defend ourselves just as well."

"But there are men here with guns," said Laura. "We would have to defend ourselves."

"I think we can do that," said Beth. "Besides, most of the men they've sent out. I don't think they've that many people defending at the moment."

"I've counted three," said Caroline. "That's not counting Robert or Tom or Doris."

"Don't forget they've got Gregory working in the kitchen," said Hazel. "So with the three at the gate, the three big wigs that makes a total of seven people here right now."

"Seven people isn't enough to keep us here," said Maggie. "Seventy people couldn't even keep us."

Laura still didn't sound convinced. "What do you suggest? Just call a taxi to take us back home? How do we really know we're in danger anyway?"

"Why did they lie to us then?" said Hazel. "Why tell us they got a message saying the boys are dead when we know that's impossible. And why is Robert so keen for us to move up with him to the top floor?"

"I have a fair idea why," said Stacey disgusted.

"How are you doing ladies?" came Tom's voice from behind.

"Oh, we're fine," mumbled Maggie, not looking at him.

"That's good," he said with a smile. He then turned towards Beth. "I'm sorry to hear that you're friends were lost. Robert told me the bad news."

"Thanks," said Beth, trying to avoid eye contact.

Tom pulled a seat from another table and sat down.

"I hear Robert is making preparations for things to be more comfortable for you."

"Er, yeah," said Beth still avoiding having to look Tom in the face.

"I understand things may be very frightening for you all. It's a lot to take in and even more to adjust to, but you must believe me this is the best place you can be. There's a massive wall surrounding us for a start which is defended around the clock. We have grounds within these walls that are big enough for children to play in." He looked down towards Eddie and Kerry and smiled. "Hopefully we'll find more children soon for you to play with, wouldn't that be good?"

"Yes," said Kerry, who like Beth, kept her gaze away from him.

"This house will hold everything we'll need," continued Tom. "There are so many floors and rooms that if one hundred people turned up today we can look after them all. Feed them, clothe them, give them shelter, entertain them and more importantly keep them all safe."

"What about the four young men who you supposedly sent out to their deaths," spat out Maggie, staring directly at Tom.

"Mum!" scolded Laura.

"That's quite all right," said Tom, patting Laura's hand. "You have ever right to be angry about that."

"You're darn right we are," said Maggie.

"Nobody is as angry as Robert in himself for allowing them to go out," said Tom. "I told him myself that perhaps they should stay a bit longer but he thought they would be safe with Frankie and Jones. It was a miscalculation that he said he will have on his conscience for the rest of his life. That is why he has being trying so hard to help make things easier for you."

"You really think staying here is the best for us?" said Maggie. "If your two men couldn't look after our boys, how can we be sure you'll be able to look after us?"

Tom stood up and looked like he was thinking long and hard. He then looked over once again towards Beth.

"There's nothing I can say that will convince you, is there?"

Beth looked nervously around at the others before finally looking up at Tom.

"It's not that we're not grateful for what you've done, because we are. It's just that we're so scared and confused we just don't know what is going on."

"That's understandable," said Tom. "Perhaps if I showed you something then maybe you can see how prepared we are and how in control we really are."

"What do you mean?" said Stacey. "Show us what?"

"It's risky to take you all, but if… Beth, is it?"

Beth nodded.

"If Beth and maybe one other of you would come with me, I'll show her why and if she's convinced, will it convince the rest of you?"

"Beth's not going anywhere without me," said Stacey, grabbing her friend's hand.

"I don't like the sound of that one bit," said Maggie angrily.

"That's also fair enough. Maybe this will show I'm serious," said Tom as he pulled out his gun and handed it to Beth. "The safety is off, all you have to do is to pull it and it will fire."

Beth looked at the gun unsure whether to take it or not.

"Trust me, Beth," he said softly. "If you don't, you can always shoot me."

Without saying a word, Beth slowly took the gun from Tom. She held it pointing down to the ground, half scared about it going off and shooting someone accidentally.

"Good," said Tom pleased. "Now if you will all wait here, Beth and her friend will come with me."

Chapter 24

"Holy shit, I don't believe it," said Arnold.

"What?" said Benny.

Arnold pointed up ahead the road where a bus was stopped.

"That's not our bus, is it?" said Benny. "It is."

"Why's it stopped?" asked Mathew.

"I don't know," said Arnold as he signalled to everyone to move off the road, and to behind a large tree.

"You reckon we could jump the two of them and take the bus," said Connor. "Leave them bastards behind and see how they like it?"

"That's exactly what I was thinking," said Arnold smiling.

"Well first of all, where are they?" said Benny. "Have they broken down or something because if they have, it's going to be no use to us."

"Kid's got a point," said Connor. "We need to know what the deal is."

"Alright, just wait here, I'll check it out," said Arnold.

"No way, Arnold. You're not going up there without us," said Benny.

"I'm just going to have a look," said Arnold standing up. "I just want to see where they are. We'll have a better chance of sneaking up if it's just one of us."

"Alright," said Benny reluctantly. "But we're not staying behind this tree here. We'll follow a few feet you behind."

"Just don't get too close, and keep an eye out for any of them red eyed bastards," said Arnold. "Wish me luck."

Before anyone could wish Arnold luck, he scurried up the road towards the bus. He crouched down when he reached the back end of it and peered round. He turned back to the others and saw they were slowly making their way to him.

"For Christ's sake," he breathed. "I told you guys to wait back."

"Now who's being taking the hero pills," said Benny. "In case you forgot, those guys had guns."

Arnold shock his head half frustrated but yet appreciative of the support. He couldn't help but try and suppress a slight smile.

"You win then," he said. "Just let me go up ahead and see if they're about. That okay?"

The three nodded together as Arnold gave a reciprocating nod back, stood up and stepped around the corner of the bus.

Out of nowhere Jonesy appeared in front of Arnold, yelled out, and fired his shotgun straight into his chest.

Arnold's body flew back as the others could only watch in horror. He then fell to the ground and lay there motionless. Jonesy stared at what he done, eyes wide and open mouthed.

"You bastard!" screamed Benny as he readied to swing his axe at Jonesy.

"I'm sorry! I'm sorry! I'm sorry!" sobbed Jonesy as he dropped his shotgun and fell to his knees. "I didn't know it was you. I thought it was them."

Jonesy then buried his head in his hands and wept. Mathew knelt down at Arnold's body and shock his head.

"I'm sorry, Benny," he said. "He's…"

"Get up!" screamed Benny, as he grabbed Jonesy by his collar and dragged him up.

"I'm sorry, I'm sorry," repeated Jonesy, as Benny pushed him up against the side of the bus and pinned the handle of his axe hard against his chest.

"Go easy on him, Benny," said Mathew. "That's not one of those things, he's a real person."

"This person just killed Arnold," snapped back Benny. "You know how many people I've lost since yesterday? Far too many."

"I'm sorry, I really am," cried Jonesy.

"Why you do it? Why?" yelled Benny.

"I didn't know. I didn't know it was him," sobbed Jonesy.

"Wait a minute. Where's the other one?" said Connor picking up the shotgun and looking around.

"Answer him!" shouted Benny, pushing the handle harder against Jonesy. "Where is he?"

"We ran out of petrol. Frankie's gone to see if he can find some," coughed out Jonesy. "He must have been gone half an hour or so."

"So why did you do it," snarled Benny again.

"I told you," blubbered Jonesy. "I didn't know it was him."

"Not that!" snapped back Benny. "Why did you leave us behind? Huh?"

"It was Frankie. I didn't want to do it, but he said we had to."

"Don't give me that shit!" shouted Benny, as he took a step back and then kicked Jonesy as hard as he could between the legs. Jonesy fell to his knees gasping.

"Benny, please…" said Mathew.

"No, he's alright," said Connor pushing Mathew back. "I want to hear this."

"Frankie said Robert told him to do it," cried Jonesy. "I don't know why but we had to make sure you helped get us much as we could, then you were taken out."

"Why?" demanded Benny.

"I said I don't know why."

"Think harder," said Connor, tapping the side of Jonesy's head with the barrel. "Why would this big Rob fella want us dead?"

Jonesy began to shake as he closed his eyes tight.

"Closing your eyes won't make us go away," said Connor pushing the barrel harder. "Now tell us!"

"Please you got to believe me. I know nothing. I just put my head down and do what I'm told. If that makes me a coward then that's what I am. I swear I don't know what's going on the most of the time. I tell you, I know nothing. Nothing, I tell you."

Benny smacked Jonesy hard to the side of the head with the bottom of the axe handle, knocking him unconscious.

"I wouldn't blame you if you hit him with the other end," said Connor as he watched Jonesy slump to the ground.

"You wouldn't, would you?" said Mathew nervously.

"No," said Benny softly. "I don't think I could."

He looked over were Arnold's body lay, and lowered his head.

"He was a good guy. Rest easy, big lad," said Connor, as he took off his jacket and placed it over the top half of Arnold's body.

"Amen," said Mathew solemnly.

"Piece of shit," muttered Connor as he looked at Jonesy's unconscious body before running onto the bus.

"What you doing?" shouted Mathew. "He said they're empty. The bus isn't going anywhere."

Connor returned from the bus holding a box of shotgun shells.

"Might need these if we want half a chance at getting back," he said.

"You know how to load these," asked Mathew.

"Pretty much. I went clay pigeon shooting on my brother's stag do. Didn't hit very many but I know how to reload them and shit like that."

"Just don't be firing too many," said Benny. "Those things are going to hear and be coming this way."

"Doubt it, Ben," said Connor as he loaded two new shells into the shotgun. "They're not smart and they're slow. Besides, we should see them coming from a mile away."

"Perhaps, but I still think we should…"

"Wait, you hear that?" interrupted Mathew. "It sounds like…"

"A car!" said Connor.

Further up the road a white transit van was making its way towards them.

"Should we flag it down?" asked Mathew. "They could give us a ride back."

"Just be careful, we don't know if they're going to be friendly," said Benny.

"We'll hide round the side here while Mathew gets their attention," said Connor.

"Why me?" said Mathew, as he watched the other two disappear behind the bus.

"They're not going to stop if they see us with a shot gun and an axe now," shouted Connor.

"Guess not," muttered Mathew.

Benny and Connor remained crouched behind the bus as they heard Mathew shout out for the van to stop. They heard the van come to a halt and then the car door open and then slam shut.

"Guys?" called Mathew.

Benny and Arnold looked up to see Mathew slowly walking round the back corner of the bus.

"I'm sorry, guys, I didn't know," he said.

"Know what?" said Benny.

"Nice to see you boys too!"

"Aw shit," said Connor, when he saw Frankie appearing with a shot gun pointed at Mathew's head.

Chapter 25

"What's in here?" asked Stacey as Tom unlocked a door on one of the many floors of the house.

"Hopefully something to convince you to stay, I hope," he replied.

Through the door was a large room covered in darkness, which lit up when Tom flicked a switch at the side.

"Voila," he said. "Welcome to the Aladdin's cave of survival in the new world."

Beth and Stacey looked around the room opened mouthed.

All around the room were shelves stacked with cans of soup and beans, cereal packets, bottled drinks, flour, sugar, tea, coffee and other things found in a general food store.

"That's not all," said Tom as he walked over to a wall of cupboards and opened both doors wide of the first one. Inside on the shelves were half a dozen hand guns and a shot gun with a stack of boxes beneath, presumably filled with ammunition.

"We do have a lot more weapons but they're out with the men on the buses currently," continued Tom as he closed the cupboard door. "We like to keep a few at home just in case we end up needing them here."

"For what?" asked Stacey.

"For whatever is thrown at us," laughed Tom as he walked over to the opposite wall, also with a row of cupboards. He open one and inside was packed with bandages, bottles of medicine and other medical equipment. "We're more than prepared. This is just the tip of the iceberg. All these other cupboards are filled with what we need."

He once again closed the cupboard. "I sense you're still not totally convinced," he said. "Trust me, we have a few other tricks up our sleeves. Take this one for example."

Tom pulled out of his pocket the black device he had used on the bus the day before.

"What is that?" asked Stacey.

"That detects them, doesn't it?" said Beth as Tom handed it to Stacey.

"You're not just a pretty face," laughed Tom.

"Er, thanks," replied Beth, as she looked over Stacey's shoulder. "How does it work?"

"You would need to speak to Robert about that. They're his invention. I'm just grateful they do their job. Certainly helped us yesterday."

Stacey noticed the 'on' button on the side and held it down.

"So what is the story with Robert anyway? How come he knows so much," she asked.

Before Tom could give an answer the device began to bleep. Beth and Stacey looked up in shock at Tom, who calmly took it off Stacey and turned it off.

"Don't worry about it beeping here," said Tom with a slight hint of nervousness in his voice. "It's just picking up…"

"What?" exclaimed Beth and Stacey together.

"Something else," he mumbled as he placed the device back in his pocket.

"Something else?" said Beth.

Tom paused for a moment and then sighed.

"Okay, ladies, you win," he said smiling. "Robert's probably going to kill me for telling you, but what the heck."

Beth and Stacey both looked at each other apprehensively. They turned back to Tom to see him dragging a two and a half foot tall metal cylinder, from under a table and up onto a bench at the side.

"Uncle Robert's secret recipe," he said, trying his best to hide the fact that lifting the cylinder had taken some effort.

"What's in there?" said Beth, gingerly walking closer to it.

"Holy water," said Tom with a grin.

"What? Actual holy water like you get in church."

"Well, yes and no," said Tom. "Once again, Robert is the person to speak to about how it's made exactly. But what he tells me, it is blessed water which Robert has specially prepared."

"You don't know, do you?" said Beth.

Tom laughed.

"You really are a smart one. Truth be told you're right. Robert has been a God send for us here and I'm just glad he came to us with all his gifts and knowledge."

Tom unscrewed the top of the cylinder and placed it down on the table. He then dipped his hand into it and then held it out for the two girls to see.

"Perfectly safe for us, but any of those turned people will find it most unpleasant. Fatal even."

"So if we were to head into a church or something we'll be safe," said Beth.

"It's a bit more to it than that. Robert has added something to it to make it something different. Here, it has a certain smell of it."

"I'll take your word on that," said Beth recoiling from Tom's hand.

"Sorry," said Tom realising Beth wasn't keen on the idea of sniffing his hand. "I can get over excited sometimes. We're at the centre of something massive in the history of mankind. We all should be honoured."

"So how much of this holy water do you have?" asked Stacey. "Do we have enough to build a moat or something around here?"

"I'll have to ask Robert about that."

'What a surprise,' thought Beth to herself.

"He makes it behind this door," said Tom pointing behind him towards the far end of the room.

"And where does he get the holy water from?" said Beth.

"The same way everyone does. They bless it themselves. Remember one of the people we picked up before you was a priest? He is working with Robert to help make it to keep us all safe."

"Now that you mention it, I don't recall seeing him since we arrived last night," said Beth.

"Yeah," said Stacey. "He wasn't down for breakfast or lunch and I haven't seen him between then either."

"Robert and him must be very busy preparing this all for us," said Tom as he proudly patted the canister. "Don't underestimate how important this new and improved dihydrogen monoxide will be to us."

"I hope so," said Beth. "So why does it set off your alarm?"

"Excuse me?"

"The device you have that detects them things. What makes it go off?"

Tom looked confused at Beth for a few seconds before looking like he just remembered something important.

"Oh yes, um, well to be perfectly honest, you'd have to ask…"

"Tom. I hope you're not taking these young ladies places were they shouldn't be?"

They all turned around to see Robert standing in the doorway with his arms folded.

"Ah, Robert, I didn't see you standing there," said Tom walking towards him. "No, I'm just showing these two fine young ladies how well prepared we all are."

"And has Tom convinced you that you are indeed in the best place to be?" said Robert looking over at Beth and Stacey.

"Um, yes," said Beth who then slightly nudged Stacey.

"Oh yes. Definitely," added Stacey.

"Good," said Robert as a big grin appeared on his face. "We will have to start getting the upstairs rooms ready for you, and don't worry about that family. We'll get a room in the house sorted for them also."

"Thanks," said Beth, trying her hardest to sound like she meant it.

"Don't even mention it. Now if you will excuse us, I wish to discuss some things with Tom here. Please rejoin your friends and tell them they have nothing to worry about any more." Robert stood back from the door and allowed both girls to pass through to the corridor. He smiled at them both then disappeared further into the room with Tom. The two girls walked together down towards the lift at the end of the corridor.

"What you thinking, Beth?"

"I'm still not sure, to be honest. Maybe Tom isn't as bad as I first though, but Robert gives me the creeps."

"Yeah, I really don't want to move up to the top floor with him at all."

"Me neither. Still not sure what we should…"

"Beth, what's wrong?"

"Damn, I still have the gun Tom gave me," said Beth as she pulled it from her pocket. She looked back towards the corridor they had just walked from. "I better give it back to him I suppose. Wait here."

Beth walked back towards the room with Stacey following behind.

"Maybe give it back later, Beth," said Stacey. "He's probably busy."

"It won't take a sec," said Beth entering the store room. "Tom! You better take this back. Tom?"

There was no answer. The only people in the room were Beth and Stacey.

"They were definitely in here. Where did they go?" whispered Stacey.

"They must have gone through there," said Beth pointing to the door at the back. She walked slowly towards it.

"Beth! Don't!" gasped Stacey.

Beth ignored Stacey and turned the handle of the door and gentle pushed it slightly ajar.

"Beth! Seriously!"

"I'm just going to have a quick look. Don't worry, I'm not going to do anything stupid."

Beth slowly peered her head around the door which lead into a short corridor with a pair of steel doors on both sides and another door at the opposite end. There was still no sign of either Tom or Robert. Slowly she crept down the corridor until she reached the first door on the right. Once up close she noticed there was a small hatch in it, like she imagined prison cells would have. She reached up and gently turned the latch, releasing the metal flap. She peered inside.

"Jesus!" she exclaimed as she jumped back. Inside were two people, a man and a woman, both wearing the familiar black trousers, white shirt uniform of the sanctuary, who were walking around the small cell aimlessly. It was when the man turned around and Beth saw the pair of red eyes that made her jump. She quickly closed the hatch and turned to Stacey.

"This isn't right, this isn't right at all."

"I don't like it here," said Stacey breathing uneasily. "You're right. Let's get the others and just get out of here. Go back to Maggie's house and stay there."

Suddenly there was a single muffled gun shot that came from behind the door at the far end of the corridor.

"What was that?" said Stacey

Beth never answered but slowly walked towards the door.

"Beth! You said you weren't going to do anything stupid! I think this might qualify!"

"I'm just going to listen. Somebody could be in trouble."

Stacey rolled her eyes, while yet knowing Beth was doing the morally right thing.

Beth held her ear to the door and strained to listen.

"Can you hear anything," whispered Stacey.

"I'm not sure," said Beth. She took her head away from the door, looked at the gun in her hand then over to Stacey.

"No, you can't go in there," pleaded Stacey. "You've no idea what's behind there. Let's just get the others and go. Now."

Before Stacey could reply the door opened wide, and Robert appeared, his arms and front soaking wet.

"What the hell are you two doing here?" he demanded as he nearly knocked them over before he could see them.

Beth and Stacey both looked at him dumbstruck, unable to think of an answer.

"Well?" he replied snappily.

"T-tom," stuttered Beth. "He lent me his gun and I wanted to give it back."

Robert looked at her apprehensively for a few moments that for Beth felt like an hour.

"That all?" he said.

"Yes, here it is," said Beth as she held out the gun for him.

"I guess that's all right then," said Robert a little more calmly as he took the gun off Beth. "It's not safe this area of the house for people to wander around unguided. Tom really should have been more…

"Oh my God!" shrieked Stacey as she held her hands to her mouth. Beth quickly turned to see what was wrong, and saw that Stacey was looking past Robert, into the room he had come out of. She looked over and could see a large circular tank, barely a foot high in the middle of the room filled with what looked like water.

And at the far side of the tank, was Tom's lifeless body, leaning over the side with his head submerged under the water.

"He's dead, isn't he? You killed him," yelled Stacey.

Robert then pointed the gun that Beth had just given him at her forehand and then produced another gun from his side which he pointed at Stacey.

"Girls, girls, girls," he said sighing. "I really wish you didn't see that."

Chapter 26

"So you going to shoot us then?" said Beth.

"I really don't want to but that's really down to you two," replied Robert, still keeping his aim on the two girls.

"What do you mean?" asked Stacey, looking nervously at the gun directed at her.

"If you behave yourselves and fall in line like the others, you will be kept safe. Treated very well even."

"Just like Tom did?" said Beth.

"Tom is, how you say, collateral damage. Just like the millions of others who have died the world over. There's no difference."

"Except that you killed him," shouted Beth. "There's a world of difference."

Robert smiled. "You're a feisty one. I like that." With a wave of the pistol, he signalled both of them to come through to the room. "Tom's death was a sacrifice to give the rest of us a better chance to survive in this new world."

"You drowned him! How does that help anyone?" shouted Beth. "Whatever I thought of Tom, it was nothing compared to what you are. You're just one twisted sick bastard."

"It may look that way, my dear, but I assure you there is method in the madness." Robert then sat at the edge of the vat of water. "I take it Tom told you about the special holy water that we are brewing here?"

"Please tell me that's not the water you just drowned him in? How the hell is that holy water?" said Beth with a hint of disgust in her voice.

"The very same, my dear. You think reciting a simple prayer or mumble a few words is enough? It takes a lot more than that. Believe me, I have seen what we are up against and it is going to take the very soul of a believer, infused in this water, to make it as holy as possible."

"You really are mad," said Stacey in amazement. "How can that possibly be right?"

"Well, a few other processes are then required to add to it," replied Robert, pointing with his head to shelves on the far wall, full of bottles with various chemicals and liquids.

"The priest who was on the bus last night with us," said Beth. "You killed him here too?"

"I don't like the word killed," said Robert. "Sacrificed is a much better term. But yes, if you wish to describe it that way. If it makes you feel any better, Tom had no idea what was going on within this room. He, like you, foolishly believed that a few words were enough and had no idea the process involved. I assure you his suffering was kept to a bare minimal."

"You're actually murdering priests to make holy water? That's insane," said Stacey.

"Actually he was the first one. Hopefully I'll not need any more after Tom has given his life for the cause."

"The other people know about this as well?" asked Beth.

"They are none the wiser. I don't think they would understand to be honest. They're not smart people, like you two ladies."

He looked at the two girls, waiting for an answer. Stacey and Beth looked at each other, then stared back at him.

"Who are you?" said Beth eventually, looking at him bewildered.

"Who I was before this began is no longer important. Granted, it was because of who I was and where I worked that I was able to foresee and prepare for what happened, but this is a new world we are living in. A new world where I am the saviour. A world where my people will be safe and well looked after."

"I think Maggie was right all along," said Beth loudly to Stacey. "He is a nutcase."

"A nutcase?" said Robert angrily. "Have you seen what it's like out there and how good it could be living here with me? You could have it all. You wouldn't have to work and scrape by with the others. You'd be living at the top, with me sharing the privileged life that I have carved out."

"Forget it," said Beth. "There's no way I'm going to live up there as your wife or whatever you call it. I do have standards and you fall well below."

"Er, Beth," whispered Stacey. "I don't want to be his wife, but I don't want to be shot either."

"He's not going to shoot us," said Beth staring at Robert defiantly. "He's going to let us and the others leave here. "

"You sure?" said Stacey.

"Positive. People are going to notice us missing if he does. It will be easier for him if we all just left without any fuss. Be a lot easier than trying to dispose of two bodies."

"Don't be so bold," laughed Robert. "Disposing of bodies isn't that difficult. I already got rid of the priest this morning. You didn't happen to look in at some of the residents in the side rooms, did you?"

"You don't mean…" gulped Stacey.

"They're a hungry lot and I'm sure Tom will help fill a hole in my test subjects' stomachs. I really would have preferred to have kept you two ladies up with me but I guess it's not to be. I'll just have to convince that other girl in your group. Caroline, is it? And perhaps the woman with the two children? Maybe they'll call me daddy?"

"You bastard!" shouted Beth. "You leave them alone."

"You're in no position to make demands, especially after you turned down my very generous offer," sneered Robert. "This is my house now and I will run it as I please, and since you have turned down my generous hospitality, I think you've out stayed your welcome."

Two gun shots were then fired in quick succession.

Chapter 27

"You little bastards, you killed him," yelled out Frankie noticing Jonesy lying on the ground.

"Calm down, he's still alive," said Connor. "Unfortunately, I might add."

"He better be," said Frankie, gently nudging him with his foot while keeping his gun pressed against Mathews head. "And you better keep back, or I'll blow this little bitch's head clean off."

"You killed one of ours," replied Connor. "So if we did kill him we'd be even."

"Is that right, son?" said Frankie glaring at Connor. "How about you shut that bloody mouth of yours and start loading the goods from the bus into my van here?"

"And then what?" shouted Benny. "You going to drive off and leave us here again?"

"Don't take it personally, boys," said Frankie with a fake smile. "Boss's orders. He wanted us to take you out here and put a couple of bullets in your heads but I thought this way was a little more humane. Besides, bullets are worth saving."

"What? Why? Why did he want us dead?" said Benny.

"He didn't think your faces fitted. You'd be trouble."

"Trouble? What you mean trouble?" said Connor "Did he think we'd make prank phone calls and piss on the toilet seat or something?"

"Trouble as you wouldn't be so keen adjusting to the chain of command and the way things would be for you."

"You're not making much sense, asshole," said Benny. "Get to the point. Why get rid of us?"

A wicked grin came across Frankie's face.

"You're not going to like this but well, you did ask. Robert plans to rebuild the world starting at our humble little home. There's going to be guys at the bottom who did the grunt work and then there's guys at the top who run the show and reap all the rewards. Kinda like real life, eh?"

"Go on," said Benny impatiently.

"Tom, the guy who owns that place hasn't got a set of balls so Robert has set himself up at the top of the tree. And being at the top gives you first choice on all the best food, drink, cigars and…heh, woman."

Frankie chuckled when he saw the expressions on the boys' faces.

"Seems Robert has his eye on your two girlfriends. I wouldn't be surprised if he's giving it to them right now."

Benny gritted his teeth and clenched his axe tighter. "And you're happy with that? Allow him to get away with it while you kiss his ass?"

"Oh no, Robert's a fair man and he knows to reward loyalty. I've my eye on the little fat vampire girl we got back there. I'd love to try and crack a smile on her sour little face."

"You sick bastard!" shouted Benny. "I will kill you! Literally! I will kill you!"

"Oh don't worry, I'll make sure the others don't feel left out. Also like that other blonde girl. What's her name? Picked her up along with this boy here."

He prodded Mathews head with the barrel several times.

"Talking to you, boy," he said gruffly. "What's the name of your little bitch?"

"Caroline," said Mathew closing his eyes tight and biting his lip.

"Caroline, eh? That's a pretty name for a nice pretty girl. I'm sure she can be a dirty one in the sheets. Am I right, eh? Come on, lover boy. Spill the beans. What's she like when she's horny?"

"I-I-I," stuttered Mathew.

"You haven't done it with her?" exclaimed Frankie with excitement. "Oh this is even better. Old Frankie here is going to make sure she'll never forget her first time."

Frankie let out a huge laugh but in a spilt second later, it turned into a gasp of pain. While he had been mouthing off, Mathew had pulled out his knife, spun in close to him and stuck it deep into his side.

"Mathew, Move!" shouted Benny as he charged towards Frankie, holding the axe high. He swung it downwards when he got close enough, hitting Frankie in the foot and on through to the ground. Frankie dropped his shotgun and screamed even louder as Benny pulled the axe from the ground, then head-butted him. He fell back, ending up lying horizontal while half of his detached foot remained in a vertical position.

Frankie continued yelling out while staring in disbelief at his missing foot. Benny stood over him and held the blade of the axe along the bridge of his nose. He then raised it over his head and brought it crashing down towards Frankie's head, who could only shut his eyes and wait for the inevitable.

"Give us the keys to your van now," growled Benny.

Frankie opened his eyes, confused that he could still hear Benny. He turned his eyes to his left and could see the axe embedded into the ground just an inch away from his head.

"Don't make me ask again," said Benny as he pulled the axe out and raised it up once again."

"They're in the van," said Frankie shielding his face with his arms. "Just take them!"

"We will," said Benny stepping over him. "Don't forget your knife, Mathew."

"Oh yeah, right," said Mathew, kneeling down and taking a firm hold of the handle sticking out of Frankie. He yanked it out causing Frankie to once again cry out in pain.

"Oh don't be such a big baby," said Connor patting Frankie on the side of the face.

"Come on, Connor," called Benny as he got into the driver's seat in the van. "We need to move. I see a few of them coming up this way."

Connor looked up and saw there were three red eyes slowly heading towards the bus.

"Don't be hanging around here too long, pal," said Connor as he picked up the shotgun that Frankie had dropped. "Looks like you've company."

"What? No, please! You can't leave me here! Please! You can't!"

"Bet you we can," said Connor as he walked off holding a shotgun in each hand. He opened the side door of the van, placed one of the shotguns inside, and then joined Benny and Mathew in the front.

"Alright, Benny. Ready when you are," he said as he closed the door.

Benny took one final glance over at Arnold's body, and then started the van as Frankie continued to plead frantically for his life.

"Hang on," he said putting the car in gear and hitting the accelerator. "We need to get back there fast. The girls are in danger."

Chapter 28

Blood spattered out of Robert's chest as he fell backwards into the vat of water.

"You're not touching those girls," shouted an older woman. Beth and Stacey turned around to see Doris standing in the doorway holding a gun.

"You girls okay?" she asked lowering her weapon.

"Yes, thank you," said Beth.

"You think he's dead?" said Stacey watching the water in the pool turn red.

"I've never fired a gun before. Here, take this off me." said Doris shaking and handing the gun over to Beth.

"You okay?" asked Beth as Doris leaned against the door frame and closed her eyes.

"I'm fine," she said, taking deep breaths. "I just wish I had done something earlier. I had a bad feeling about him from the start and I should have done something back then."

"You've stopped him now, that's the important thing," said Beth.

"So what do we do now," said Stacey. "Do we stay here still?"

"Nooo!"

The three startled females turned around to see Robert still alive, rising up from the bloodied water.

"I'll kill you all," he growled as he stumbled to the edge and picked up one of the hand guns he dropped. Beth grabbed Stacey and pushed her through the door into the corridor out of harms way. She turned back around to grab Doris but before she could hold of her, Robert had fired off five shots. The first four struck her in the chest with the final one hitting her in the side of the head.

"Oh God," shrieked Stacey, glancing back and seeing Doris fall to the ground.

"Just run," shouted Beth, pushing Stacey forward. She turned towards Robert who had now stepped out of the pool, and pointed the gun Doris had just given her at him. "Don't move or I'll shoot."

"Don't insult me, bitch," he sneered, the soaking from the red water making him look like a monster that had just crawled out of a tar pit. "You're not going to pull that trigger otherwise you would have done it already."

"I will! I swear I will," she said, trying and failing to hide her nerves.

"No, you won't," he snapped back, as he slowly bent down to pick up the other gun. "You're going to put that gun down and come over here!"

"Beth! Come on!" shouted Stacey from the far end of the corridor.

"Damn it!" muttered Beth as she ran into the corridor and joined Stacey.

"Get back here! Both of you!" yelled Robert as he stumbled towards the door and fell to his knees.

"Never!" screamed Beth, as she ran over to one of the steel doors. "Get out of here, Stacey!"

"What are you doing," shouted Stacey as she watched Beth pull back the bolt holding the door shut, and then pulled the door open. Inside were five very large red eye men, who once they saw Beth, moved towards her. She quickly ran to the door opposite, which she knew only had two red eyes, and opened it as well.

She quickly looked over her shoulder to see Robert now leaning against the doorframe, spitting out a mouthful of blood. "You bitch," she heard him shout as she dashed through the door that led to the store room. Soon as she was through, Stacey slammed it shut hard. Several gun shots were fired which followed by the groans of what could only been from the recently released group of red eyes.

"Beth! Stacey! What's happening?"

Both girls turned around to see Caroline and Hazel standing in the room, looking concerned.

"It's Robert," said Stacey. "He was going to kill us."

Two more gun shots were fired, which were followed by an increase intensity of the moans then followed by a blood curdling scream of agony.

"What's going on in there?" said Hazel.

Beth slowly opened the door slightly and peered through the small gap.

At the far end, she could see a huge huddle of red eyes all grouped together and hunched over something. Something human sized and shaped. Something very bloody and also very dead or dying.

"I don't think Robert's going to be a problem anymore," she said. Just as she was about to close the door she noticed two motionless red eyes lying on the ground just a few feet away from her. Seemly Robert had managed to take two of them out with him.

"Is he…dead?" gulped Caroline.

"Yeah, I'd say so," said Beth. "He's not going to be bothering us."

"You killed him?" said Hazel, almost with a hint of admiration in her voice.

Beth looked nervously at Stacey, then back at Hazel. The question bringing up a stark realisation of what had just done.

"Not…directly," murmured Beth.

Hazel looked down at the gun Beth was carrying. "You didn't shoot him?"

"No. He had some people that had turned in some cells down there. I just let them out when we were trying to get away."

"Well, death by proxy then?" said Hazel. "Hey, death by proxy. That would have been a great name for a band, don't you think?"

"Benny!" shouted out Beth, as if she remembered something important that had just momentarily forgot. "We need to find out if they're still alive."

"Yes!" said Caroline excited. "Let's get out of here and find Mathew. And the others."

"I'm up for that," said Hazel. "This place just isn't for me."

"Right, we'll get a car and head out," said Beth. "Just after we block this door up. I don't want the guys back here looking for desert."

"What's going on?" said a young man rushing in, holding a shotgun and wearing the black trousers, white shirt, black tie uniform.

"This where the gun shots came from?" he asked Beth.

"Um, yeah."

"Al! In here," he called out. A second man, also carrying a shot gun and wearing the same clothing appeared at the door. Behind him, a crowd made up of the new arrivals gathered behind him.

"What is it, Joe?" he asked.

"This girl says this is where the shots were fired, isn't that right?"

"Yes," said Beth, looking over towards the door where the feeding frenzy was taking place behind. "I wouldn't go through there though. There are some of those things in there."

There was a collective gasp from the crowd of onlookers.

"You saying there's cursed folk in here?" exclaimed one terrified woman.

"I thought this place was going to be safe," shouted an elderly man.

"Here, hold on a minute," said Maggie pushing her way through the crowd to the front. "Aren't you two supposed to be guarding the front gate? Have you left the doors open to anything to walk through?"

"Calm down, grandma," said Joe dismissively. "Stevie is still there. He'll hold them off."

"That scrawny kid?" shouted the elderly man. "If he fired a gun he'd probably paralyse himself."

"He'll be fine, now could all of you just get back now," ordered Joe. "We'll take care of this."

Maggie darted her way past and over to Beth.

"Are you alright? What happened?" she asked.

"Tom and Doris are dead. Robert killed them. He tried to kill us too," replied Beth.

"Hold on there one second," shouted Joe, overhearing Beth and Maggie. "What you mean Tom and Doris are dead?"

"I think it's pretty self-explanatory, young man," said Maggie. "Taking this Robert into your house was obviously a big mistake."

Joe turned to Maggie and before he could say anything, Al took a hold of him by the arm.

"Leave it, Joe. If there's infected people inside here we got to take care of them first."

"Infected? I thought we called them cursed?"

"Infected, cursed, turned, whatever. Does it matter what we call them?"

"Yeah, guess not."

"Listen guys, there must be about ten or so of them in there," said Beth. "Maybe we could just block the door up with…"

"Just let us take care of it," said Joe arrogantly cutting her off. "If you just go stand with the other ladies and gentlemen, me and Al will deal with them."

"Sorry about him," said Al apologetically. "He is right though. Leave this to us and we'll make sure you're all safe."

"I really think you should…" said Beth but it was falling on deaf ears. She watched as Joe opened the door wide and strolled in, with Al right behind him. Up ahead at the far end the group of red eyes were still feeding over what could only be Robert's body. Joe slowly walked closer taking aim with his shotgun.

"Why not put the kettle on for everyone?" said Al turning round to Beth. "This won't take us long. No sugar in mine and I think Joe only takes…"

Al never got to finish his sentence. From the side door a red eye woman sprung out and dug her teeth into Al's shoulder.

"Oh shit! Al!" yelled Joe as he turned around to see his friend fall to the floor with a crazed woman gnawing on top of him. He took aim at the woman's head but hesitated to pull the trigger.

"Al, I can't get a clear shot," he shouted frantically.

"I can," shouted Beth, who fired a single shot into the side of the woman's head.

"Ah, God," choked Al as he pushed the woman's body off him and then struggled to get to up. "Joe! Behind you!"

Joe spun round and saw that the commotion with Al had been noticed by a few of the red eyes who were at the edge of the group feeding off Robert.

"Nooo!" he screamed, as two of them pounced on him, knocking him flat to the ground.

"Joe!" shouted out Al as he saw several more red eyes pile on top. Beth and Hazel ran over to Al and pulled him up on his feet.

"We got to get out of here! Now!" Beth shouted as she and Hazel put an arm each over their shoulders and walked him out of the corridor and back to the others.

Once through the door, Maggie slammed it shut while several men pulled across a cupboard across the door to block it. Beth and Hazel laid Al down on the middle of the floor as blood continued to pump out from his shoulder wound.

"Stacey," shouted Beth. "Get the first aid supplies!"

"Already on it," said Stacey appearing beside them with the first aid box already opened up.

"I'm a nurse," said a woman kneeling down on the other side of Al. "We got to get this wound clean."

"Oh, okay," said Stacey dejected. "I'll just leave you to it."

"That was some shooting there," said Hazel to Beth as they stood back to allow the woman to work. "Think you might have saved that bastard's life."

"Thanks," said Beth. "But it was me who opened the doors and let them out in the first place."

"Hey, if you hadn't done that then Robert would have killed us both," said Stacey turning around. "You had to do it otherwise, well, God knows what he would have done to the others. So don't be thinking you've done something wrong, because you haven't. Robert was a bad man and he got what he deserved."

"What about Joe?" said Beth sadly. "He didn't deserve to die, did he?"

"You warned him not to go in," said Maggie joining the conversation. She put her arm around Beth. "It was his own showing off and over confidence that got himself killed, not you. Don't hold yourself responsible for things that aren't your fault, Beth."

"I guess," she said softly.

"Looks like you saved this man's life," said the nurse still working on Al. "He's going to be a bit sore but he's going to be alright."

"Thanks," said Al weakly. "I owe you one."

"Don't mention it," said Beth trying her hardest to smile.

"So what do we do now," said Stacey.

"We get Al downstairs and restrained in one of the rooms," said Beth. "Do we have rope or maybe a couple of cable ties?"

"Excuse me? What?" exclaimed Al.

"It's for everyone's safety," said Beth. "We had a friend who got bit and ended up turning afterwards. I don't know if there is a connection, but it's best not to take chances."

"Don't worry," said the nurse patting Al on the leg. "I'll make sure you quite comfortable."

"Um, okay," gulped Al.

"Now we've that taken care of, we better get planning on finding the guys," said Beth. "They could be in danger."

Chapter 29

"I don't think you should be messing with that," said Mathew watching Connor tinkering with the tracking device that Frankie had left in the van.

"I'm only having a look and see how it works," said Connor. "Wonder what sort of batteries it takes?"

Benny paid no attention to either of them. He concentrated on driving the van back to the retreat as quickly as he could. Despite having not passed his driving test yet, he handled the van well. Or so he thought until he hit a pot hole.

"Shit!" he squealed as the van bounced and skidded to the side of the road. Benny hit the brakes hard and turned the wheel, bringing the van to a halt while nearly tipping it over in the process.

"Sorry, guys," said Benny taking a deep breath, before starting the van up again and driving off at a fast but not quite as fast as before speed.

"Where did that thing go?" said Connor looking down.

"What?" said Mathew.

"The tracker. I dropped it. Wait there it is."

"Still working is it?" asked Mathew as he watched Connor picking it up off the floor.

"Not sure," he replied, examining it closely. "The casing's been cracked and… wait a minute, is that blood?"

"Blood?" said Mathew.

"Yeah, blood," said Connor as he tilted the device so a trickle of blood poured out from a crack.

"What the hell?" exclaimed Benny as he did his best to watch Connor and keep his eye on the road.

Connor banged the device on the edge of the dashboard several times, making the small crack in the device bigger.

"Connor! You're getting some on me," shouted Mathew as drips of blood splashed on him.

"Sorry," he said insincerely, as he then prised open the casing. "Holy shit!"

"What the hell is that?" said Benny, eyes still half on the road and half towards Connor.

"I don't know," said Connor.

Inside the device, amongst the maze of wires, transistors and circuit boards, was what looked like a small bloody piece of raw meat. A piece of meat that was ever so slightly contracting back and forth as if it was breathing.

"That's not right," said Mathew. "That's not right at all."

"You don't say," said Connor a little flustered who quickly wounded down the window beside him and threw the whole thing out. He then wound it back up and wiped his hands on the dash board. "That was just too weird."

"That might have been a handy device to have," said Mathew.

"You're welcome to go back and get it if you like," said Connor.

"Doesn't matter," said Benny. "That machine only picks up people who have changed, and at this moment, there are people more dangerous than that."

"Agreed," said Mathew. "How long you think until we get there, Benny?"

"At this rate probably ten seconds," said Connor lifting his shotgun from the dashboard. "We need a plan though to rescue the girls. This could get nasty and dangerous."

"So what's the plan to save the boys," said Stacey.

"We need to wait until some of the buses come back. They've left this place without leaving any cars or anything," replied Beth. "I guess the only thing we can do is wait."

Everyone had gathered in the canteen, bringing down most of the supplies and weapons from the store room before nailing it shut. Although the red eyes were locked in the room off the store room, it was unanimously voted that it was best to have that room as a buffer between them and the residents. Al had been taken to the male dormitory and restrained there by the somewhat keen nurse while Stevie remained as the sole guard on the gates.

"Wait?" huffed Caroline. "How can we just wait?"

"We've no choice," said Beth. "We'll not get very far if we go out on foot. It'll be dark in a couple of hours and we know what those things are like at night."

"Beth!"

Everyone turned to see Kerry running into the canteen with her mother and brother. The little girl ran up to Beth and hugged her at tight as she could.

"I don't want you to go again" said Kerry bursting into tears. "Never, ever, ever!"

"Don't worry," said Beth, holding back some tears herself. "We're going to be safe here. I promise."

"We could think about getting back to my house," said Maggie. "I'd feel more comfortable being in my own home and what happens when the men who were sent out come back and find out Robert and the others are dead?"

"Don't be silly, mother," whispered Laura as not to upset the children. "There's a large wall around this place and there's everything we need here."

"But when the men come back?" said Maggie.

Laura sighed "I don't think they're that bad. They were just doing what Robert told them. He's gone now."

"Yes, but can we still trust them?" said Caroline. "They look like the sort that doesn't need any encouragement to do cause trouble."

"Listen everyone," said Beth firmly. "Let's just remain calm. When the men come back we'll think of a story to explain what happened to Robert and the others. We'll say there was a breach and we were attacked."

"Okay and then what?" said Caroline impatiently.

Before Beth could answer a woman ran into the canteen looking very distressed.

"There's people at the gate!" she wheezed. "They've got that young boy!"

"Who?" said Beth.

"I don't know who they are," said the woman trying hard to gain her breath. "They've got a gun pointed to that poor boys head and have threatened to shoot him if they don't get to speak to whoever's in charge."

"That will be a bit difficult," said Hazel. "Unless Gregory here is in charge by default."

"Hey, leave me out of this," said Gregory. "I just worked here as a cook. I'm no Tom or Doris."

"Well somebody better get out there and pretend to be in charge otherwise that boy is dead," said the breathless woman.

"I'll go," said Maggie.

"You're not going alone. I'm coming too" said Beth.

"This going to be an 'I am Spartacus' moment then?" said Hazel.

"Who?" asked Stacey.

"Never mind, let's just get out there," said Beth.

"I'm telling you now," yelled Connor holding Stevie by the neck and with the shotgun buried in his cheek. "You better get your boss out here now, or I'm going to paint the walls with this boy's brains!"

He then leaned close and whispered to Stevie.

"Now you know I'm not really going to blow your head off, but at least try and looked scared. Maybe start crying or something?"

"I'm not going to start crying," said Stevie. "Them people are going to think I'm gay."

"Oh sorry," said Connor sarcastically, "Wouldn't want to ruin your chances with the girls here, considering you're such a fine specimen of a man."

"You really think this is a good idea?" Mathew said to Benny, both who distanced themselves by ten metres back from Connor's fake hostage scenario.

"Honestly? No. But if it helps us get Beth and the others back then what choice do we have."

"What happens if they won't let them go?" asked Mathew trying to hide his nerves.

"We're about to find out, they're coming out now."

"Connor? It is you, isn't it? What the hell are you doing?" shouted Beth. "Let that kid go."

"Beth, it's us," shouted Benny. "We've come to save you!"

"Yeah!" shouted Connor, "That Robert is bad news."

"We know," said Beth. "Look, Connor. Just let the boy go. He's not going to cause you any trouble."

"Can't do that, Beth, honey," said Connor. "Somebody tell Robert to let our people go and there'll be no trouble.

"He's dead, Connor! Him, Tom and Doris are all dead. The only dangerous person here is the guy with the shotgun!"

"Oh," said Connor letting go of Stevie and lowering his gun.

"You don't need saving then?"

"No," said Beth, walking down the steps.

"You could have told me that, you little shit," Connor whispered to Stevie.

"You never asked," replied Stevie as he brushed himself down. "Besides, I wanted to see how you would do."

"We're all fine, guys. There's nothing to worry about," called Beth. "Now come inside. We've things to discuss."

Chapter 30

"Here. Get that into you," said Beth as she put down a bowl of soup in front of Benny as he sat in silence alone in the canteen.

"Thanks," he said as he just stared at it.

"Look, Benny. You've got to eat something," said Beth as she sat down opposite. "We can't let this beat us, we can't. Now please, eat."

"I would if I had a spoon."

"Oh, sorry. I'll go get you one."

Beth returned from the kitchen with a soup spoon and handed it to Benny.

"Thanks," he said with a smile and then began to eat his soup earnestly.

"You know, I didn't think much of Arnold before all this," she said as she watched Benny eat. "Thought he was your typical self-obsessed, show off prick. Guess we got to see the real Arnold in the end."

"I was starting to like him too," said Benny sadly. "He didn't deserve it. Neither did Jason or Pete."

"I know," replied Beth. She stayed silent as she watched Benny finish eating.

"That was great, Beth," he said wiping his mouth after he finished. "Good to know that you can still get a good bowl of soup despite it being the end of the world."

Beth smiled weakly.

"You really think it's the end of it all," she asked.

Benny shrugged. "It's the end of something. The end of the way things used to be perhaps?"

"Hey, what you guys up to," shouted Connor from across the hall. He walked over and sat down at the table, his hair dripping wet. "You should catch yourself a shower while you can, Ben. Not saying that you stink or anything but that hot water isn't going to last forever so get it while you can. Maybe some of us should share showers to save the hot water?"

"Where's Mathew," asked Benny. "Did he get something to eat?"

"Think him and Caroline are catching up," said Connor, nudging Benny in the ribs. "Think they've got one of the rooms in the dormitories to themselves. Fancy flashing the van headlights through the windows and piss them off?"

"Leave them be," said Beth. "God knows how many moments like that they'll have left."

"Aw, you're no fun, girl," said Connor laughing. "What you say, Benny?"

"I think I know what we have to do," said Benny.

"You see?" shouted out Connor towards Beth. "Benny's up for a laugh."

"No, not that," said Benny rolling his eyes. "I mean, I know what we need to do next?"

"I don't follow, Benny," said Beth.

"Look, there's Stacey!" shouted out Connor as he saw her walking into the hall. "Hey, Stace, come and join us!"

Connor leaned closer to Benny.

"Think she'll go for the sharing a shower idea," he whispered as he nudged Benny once again in the ribs.

"How you guys doing?" said Stacey as she joined them at the table.

"Benny's got a plan," said Connor gleefully. "Don't know what it is but I'm sure it's not as good as mine."

"Oh? What is it?" asked Stacey.

Benny cleared his throat before speaking.

"I think I know what may have caused all this. Well maybe not exactly but I think I know where we need to go."

"You certainly have a good grip of what's going on there, Ben," said Connor.

"Shush! Let him finish," scolded Beth. "Go on, Benny."

"Connor stole a tape player that Tom had acquired out in the road. Last night we got a chance to play it. Seemed it belonged to a scientist who was part of a top secret team working on some project."

"You mean they made this all happen?" said Stacey shocked. "Why?"

"No, I don't think they did," said Benny as he leaned closer to the table. "Inside this secret lab they kept some sort of, I dunno, thing."

"Thing?" said Beth. "What sort of thing?"

"A thing that has somehow caused all this to happen. You still have the player, Connor?"

"Sorry, no. It was in my jacket which I…um, lost."

"Lost?" asked Beth.

"Don't ask," said Connor, looking sidewise at Benny as he stood up and put his hand in his back pocket. "I do still have this though if you don't believe us."

"What's this?" asked Beth as Connor passed her a plastic card.

"Some sort of security card, I reckon," said Connor. "Belongs to some guy called Purcell."

Beth looked at the card, then handed it to Stacey who looked at it also before handing it over to Benny.

"We got to get to the lab that has this thing and destroy it," said Benny tapping the card on the table. "This pass should let us right in."

"Good plan, Bernard," said Connor leaning back in his seat. "There is however one little problem."

"We don't know where the secret lab is?" said Benny pre-empting the question.

"Um, yeah," said Connor.

"Except I think I do know where it is."

"Where?" said the other three altogether.

Benny couldn't help hide the smile on his face.

"This tape was picked up from the scene of an accident. An accident involving an army truck, right Connor?"

"Yeah, that's right. Yesterday."

"Beth, you remember how you said you nearly got run off the road by a couple of trucks when you were coming up to the camp."

"We were, but Benny, even if that's the same truck, that doesn't really tell us were the lab is."

"I suppose we could work out the area it could be in roughly," said Stacey. "But it's still a needle in a haystack, surely?"

"No, not all," said Benny. "Pete saw the army trucks too. In fact, he even saw them coming out of the building which I think must be the hidden lab."

"Where?" asked Beth.

"Right where our camp was. I thought Pete was bullshitting me. To be fair, I was a little hung over at the time and wasn't paying much attention to what he was saying."

"So wait, what are you saying now, Benny," said Stacey trying to take it all in. "You've found the secret lab, so what now?"

"I don't know about you guys, but I'm going to go down there in the van, get inside, find whatever's in there and then chop its stinking head off."

"You don't know if that will make any difference, Benny," said Beth. "It could be dangerous."

"I know it's dangerous," replied Benny. "In fact I fully expect it to be dangerous and would be a little disappointed if it wasn't. But the one thing I'm not going to do is sit here and just wait to die."

"Now don't you be hogging all the glory for yourself, Benny boy," piped in Connor. "If you're going anywhere it will be with me beside you."

"And I'm coming too," said Beth. "I wasn't sure if you guys were still alive at all this morning. I'm not going through that again."

"Me too," said Stacey nodding gently.

"I think we better leave first thing tomorrow morning," said Benny. "It's not long until night and we know how crazy these things can get."

"So it's agreed then," said Beth, standing up. "We wait until first light tomorrow."

"Sounds like a plan," said Connor. "I'll round up some ammo and fun stuff and stick it in the van."

"I'll give you a hand," said Beth. "We should make sure the guys here have enough left to defend themselves."

"I'm going to have a walk around and check a few things out," said Benny, also standing up. "I want to make sure this place is secure for the night."

Benny stood outside the boarded up door to the store room. He pushed his ear up to the door, and along with the loud banging and thuds, he could hear a familiar haunting chant.

"*Waaan Theee Zerro Kay Zerro Aree!*"

"Hey, Benny!"

Benny turned to see Mathew walking up the corridor towards him.

"Hi, Mathew," said Benny. "What's up?"

"Beth told me to see if you needed a hand with anything. What you doing?"

"Just a bit concerned about this room here," said Benny as he gently pulled at the boards nailed across the door. "Beth said it was used as a store room which had a couple of rooms off it."

"Those the rooms which have a couple of them things locked

up? Caroline told me about it. That sounds messed up if you ask me."

"Yeah, just a bit," said Benny, looking down the opposite direction and spying a sturdy bookcase. "Here, give me a hand moving this across the door."

"Sure," said Mathew.

The two of the grabbed the bookcase, one at each side with Benny pulling and Mathew pushing. It was quite an effort and a lot heavier than it looked, possibly helped by the large collection of weighty books filling the shelves.

"There. That should do it," announced Benny, once the door was covered completely.

"Think we might have ruined the carpet in the process," said Mathew looking at the accidental carnage they had done to the floor.

"The very least of our problems, I'd say. Don't think they'll be sending a bill to me."

"Oh, Beth told me to also tell you that a few of the men here have taken a couple of guns and are going to guard the gate tonight. Stevie wanted to do it but Maggie said he needed a break."

"Probably still needs to recover after what Connor did to him," said Benny. "Makes you wonder how thing would have gone down if it turned out Robert was still alive and holding the girls hostage."

"Certainly does. Connor's a good guy really. I know he wouldn't really have harmed him."

"Yeah, I know. He reminds me a lot of a friend of mine."

"Listen, Benny. There's something I need to ask you. I heard you and Connor and the two girls are leaving in the morning to go to this secret lab. That's the one on the tape we listened to last night, wasn't it?"

"Yes, the same one and I think I know where it's at. If my guess is right, then we'll get to the heart of all this."

"Benny, I've spoken to Caroline and we have decided we want to come with you."

"You sure you both want to? I've honestly no idea what we're going to expect and it could be the most dangerous thing we've done. That's why we don't want to round up anyone who can carry a gun and march off down there. It could be a total suicide mission for all we know."

"Yes, we're both aware of that. I've been out there with you and I know what it's like. I can help, I really think I can. I don't want to sit here, hiding in this ivory tower while you and the others are risking your lives for us. Maybe for everyone in the country. And maybe even the world."

"But, Mathew, do you really want to risk bringing Caroline with you?"

"To be honest, I'd rather she stayed here," sighed Mathew. "But after this morning, there's no way she'll have me out of her sight again. Also, I think she really wants to help."

"You really sure you want to do this? We'll not get half way and you'll want to go back?"

"We'll not do that, I swear, Benny. We're here until the end."

"Okay then," replied Benny, giving Mathew a friendly punch in the arm. "Welcome aboard the mission. Better catch yourself some sleep. We head out first thing in the morning."

The morning came quick and without much incident. No red eyes approached the gates through the night, much to the disappointment of the men on the gate, who were slightly eager to try out the shot guns.

"Wake up, Benny."

"Huh?"

"It's time to get going," said Connor, shaking Benny by the shoulder. "You didn't sleep in the van all night did you?"

"Didn't get much sleep to be honest," said Benny as he rubbed his eyes and straightened up in the seat. "How about you?"

"Maybe an hour or so. Beds in the women's block aren't much better."

"What were you doing there, or should I not ask?"

"No, nothing like that. None of them are in the mood for it anyway. I didn't fancy sharing the room with Matt and his bird."

"Oh right, I see," said Benny. "Speak of the devil."

"Hey guys, we're ready when you are," shouted Mathew as he and Caroline approached the van.

"You still sure you want to come along?" said Benny. "It's not too late to change your mind."

"You're not going to get rid of us that easy," said Mathew.

Beth, Stacey and Maggie appeared at the front door

"Are you sure you don't want to stay and have some breakfast," asked Maggie. "You'll need to keep your strength up."

"We'll be fine, Maggie. Thank you," said Beth. "We'll eat on the road. Best to head on and make the most of the daylight."

"You don't want to say goodbye? Even to Kerry? She adores you, you know?"

Beth closed her eyes tight and took a deep breath.

"I know. I just don't think she'd understand. It was hard enough trying to convince Hazel to stay here and look after the others."

"I'm going to make sure she comes back," said Stacey putting her arm round Beth.

"I know you will," said Maggie putting on a brave smile. "Just make sure you all come back."

"I promise," said Beth has she leaned forward and hugged Maggie tight. "Tell Kerry I've just gone out to bring back ice cream or something."

"You're going to have some explaining to do when you come back and you haven't got any," said Maggie laughing while trying to hold back tears. She then let go and turned to Stacey and hugged her.

"You girls be careful," she said. "And make sure them boys don't do anything stupid. You know what men are like when they get together."

"We're ready when you all are," called Benny opening the side door of the van. "Connor and Mathew are going to ride shotgun up with me in the front. You ladies don't mind being in the back?"

"So how come you guys get to ride shotgun then?" asked Beth.

"Cause I have a shotgun," said Connor with a cheesy grin and holding his gun up high.

"Oh, put it away, you're not impressing anyone," joked Beth as she stepped into the back of the van, followed by Stacey then Caroline.

"Don't forget what I told you," said Maggie as Connor closed the side door. She turned to Connor and whispered "You men be careful too. Keep those girls safe."

"I will," said Connor and before he knew it Maggie had leaned in and hugged him.

"You're good men. I can tell," she said. "We'll all be praying for you back here."

"Thanks," said Connor.

"You sure you don't want him to stay with you, Maggie?" shouted Benny with a laugh.

"Ha bloody ha, Benny. I'm coming now." said Connor, as he placed the shotgun on the dashboard and got in the passenger seat alongside Mathew.

Benny turned around and looked at the girls huddled in the back of the van.

"Ready, ladies?"

All three nervously nodded. He then turned to Mathew and Connor.

"Gentlemen?"

"Let's do this," said Mathew.

Maggie signaled to the men guarding the gate to open it. They opened it and as soon as the van passed through, they closed it again.

Maggie watched as they disappeared into the horizon. She closed her eyes and prayed.

"Please, God. Let them have a chance."

Chapter 31

It was strange returning back to the camp site. It was only a few days since they were last there but so much had happened. As they turned up into the familiar road, Connor leaned out the window and took several shots at a group of red eyes, wandering along aimlessly.

"I'm getting better at this I reckon," he said with a huge grin. He looked at the others who were not showing his enthusiasm. "Suit yourselves," he muttered.

"You okay, Benny?" asked Beth as he drove into the main camp area. There were only a few red eyes dotted about the area, a far cry from the scene when they were last there.

"Yeah, I will be," he said as he stopped the van by the cabin and got out. He lifted the axe from the car dash board and strutted over to the nearest red eye. The red eye turned as Benny approached and once it noticed him, it reached out to lunge at him. It didn't get far as Benny had the axe already high above his head which he then brought down through its head, splitting the red eye into two halves.

"Still works," he called over to the others. "Make sure that cabin's clear then get inside! I'll clear out here!"

"Don't hog all the fun now," said Mathew pulling out his knife.

"Mathew? What are you doing?" gasped Caroline, as she watched Mathew run over to a red eye and shove the knife through its eye socket. He took a firm grip of the back of its head then wiggled the knife in as far as it would go. Blood flowed from the eye as the red eye shock for a brief moment, then stopped. Mathew yanked the knife out and let the red eye drop to the ground.

"There's another four still left," he said pointing them out to Benny.

"I got them," said Benny as he prepared to swing his axe again. This time he swung horizontally and decapitated one of them completely in one go.

"Nice work, guys," said Connor making his way towards the cabin. He pushed the door open with the barrel of his gun and walked in. "Anyone here?"

A groan came from the other side of the room, and a tall skinny woman appeared from the shadows. She staggered over towards Connor with her arms held out.

"Let's see those beautiful red eyes of yours," he said as he raised the gun towards the red eyes head. He pulled the trigger and the head exploded, leaving a headless corpse stagger back two steps, before falling back against the wall.

"You really should be saving your bullets," said Beth from behind, gun drawn.

"Where's the fun in that," replied Connor as he watched Beth walk into the first bedroom.

"All clear here," she shouted, as she came out and entered the second bedroom.

"Clear?" said Connor.

"Yeah," said Beth coming back out the door.

"That seems to be it safe now," said Stacey, peering round into the kitchen area. "Benny and Mathew are taking care of few out there."

"I was kind of expecting a lot more of them to be honest," said Connor, looking out the back window.

"So was I," said Beth. "There were dozens of them out here. They couldn't have just left, could they?"

"Guess that means we got a bit of time to relax then?" said Connor taking a seat and putting his feet up. "Maybe a beer or two?"

"We can't do that," said Benny, appearing at the door with his bloodied axe.

"Why not?" asked Connor.

"We haven't time. We got to get in there before it gets dark and those things get really dangerous. We haven't got Tom's super safe fortress to hide in."

"Fair enough," sighed Conner as he up got off his seat slowly. "Just get the weapons sorted and head off then?"

Mathew appeared at the door with Caroline behind him. He wiped the bloody mess of his knife on the curtains.

"That's the last of them, Benny. How much of that magic holy water do we still have?"

"Not as much as I would have liked," said Benny. "Connor, give those shotguns bullets a final soaking just to be sure. How many you got left?"

"Let's see," he said as he pulled out the box of shells from his inside pocket. He opened it and quickly counted to himself.

"About fifteen or so. How many bullets you reckon is in Beth's gun?"

"I've no idea," she said. "I'll just keep pulling the trigger until it stops. I think we better use the water for the axe and knife."

"There's nothing else here we can use?" asked Caroline. "You don't have any knives or anything?"

"I don't think so," said Stacey. "We only care up here for a party. All the guys brought up was beer, food and more beer."

"Mathew," called Benny. "We'll bring in the canister and get the weapons sorted. We'll move out as soon as we've done that."

"You did say you had beer, didn't you?" said Connor, but Benny along with Mathew had both left without answering him. He looked towards the girls but was greeted with disapproving looking from all three of them.

"Ah , hell, ladies. A condemned man can't have a last drink?" Benny and Mathew both left the cabin, narrowly avoiding stepping on one of the corpses on the ground that they hadn't noticed earlier.

"That wasn't you, was it?" asked Mathew.

"No, it was already there. Must have been Jason or Arnold."

"Who's Jason?"

"He was my brother. He died just over there." Benny pointed at the spot but didn't look.

"I'm sorry, Benny. Forgive me."

"Don't worry, you didn't know," said Benny as he opened the van door and pulled out the canister. "Grab the other end and we'll get this in the cabin."

Together Benny and Mathew brought it across while still looking around for any stray red eyes.

"You think we've got a chance of turning this all around?" said Mathew.

Benny accidentally took a glance in the direction where he last saw Jason. A bloody pile marked the spot which seemed to consist of the jacket that his brother was wearing. He turned his head quickly before he could take any more of the sight in.

"We got to try," he said doing his best to compose himself again. "If we don't do it, no one else will."

Beth held the door open for them both, and as soon as they got inside, she slammed it shut.

"So what you got planned then" said Stacey. "We need a plan, right?"

"We walk in there, we kick ass, we save the day," butted in Connor. "How's that for a plan?"

"The best one we have," said Benny as he unscrewed the top of the canister. "Who's first?"

Conner lifted the box of shotgun shells out of his pocket, and then poured them all into the canister. He looked at the group around him and shrugged his shoulders.

"Every little bit helps," he said as he reached in and pulled them out one by one.

"Me next, if that's okay with everyone," said Mathew dipping his knife in. He looked over at Caroline who was doing her best to contain her tears. "It will be fine, Caroline. Trust me."

"I know, Mathew," she said before bursting into tears. Mathew took the knife out, placed it on the table and hugged Caroline.

"Beth?" said Benny, motioning to her gun. "You want to dip your gun in?"

"Best not. I can't imagine submerging a gun in water would be good for it."

"Yeah, you're probably right," he said putting the axe down on the floor. He then tipped the canister and poured the water onto it. Once finished he set the canister upright and picked the axe back up.

"That's us then?" he said, holding the axe with authority. The group all looked at each other, then to Benny and nodded their heads.

"Lead the way, Benny," said Connor raising his shotgun above his head. "One way or another, all this stupid crap ends today."

Chapter 32

"So that's where they all went," said Beth, as she watched from behind a large oak tree.

"Great," sighed Connor. "How are we going to even get near that place now?"

They had easily found the building which Pete had spied a few days earlier. There wasn't even a single red eye on the way from the camp down the trail towards the building. However, surrounding the solid brick wall that went all the way around the grounds of the building, were lots and lots of red eyes, banging and bumping against it. From the side they were looking at, there must have been close to a hundred and there was no telling how many there were on the other sides.

"Are they guarding it or trying to get in themselves?" asked Stacey.

"Dunno," replied Connor. "Can't imagine they're going to let us walk over and hop in either way."

"Where's the gate in," said Mathew. "Your friend, Pete was it? Did you say he saw army trucks drive out of this place?"

"Must be on the other side," said Benny. "The wall around that place looks quite high. Going through a gate might be our best chance."

"That won't be easy," said Mathew. "How do we get them things away from there for us to get up to the gate and go in?"

"And what if the gate's locked?" said Caroline. "This is just suicide."

"Let's be honest, how many more days do you think we really have left," said Connor. "Maybe we can last another night when those bastards go shit crazy, but if I don't know about you, but if we're going to die this week, at least let it be doing something almost cool and heroic."

"So any bright ideas about getting in then?" said Stacey.

"Yeah," he said, handing his shotgun to her. "Hold on to this. I've a really cool and heroic idea."

"What am I supposed to do with this?" asked Stacey puzzled. "Hey, where you going?"

"I'm going to get the van down here"

"What?!"

"It's the best way," he said, as he walked up the trail back towards the camp. "Ram the gates, jump out and get inside." Stacey watched him disappear up the trail before turning around to the others.

"He's mad. There's no way that's going to work."

"It might be our only chance," said Benny.

"And what if it doesn't work? What then?"

"We die," replied Benny. "Those things grab us, tear us apart and eat us while we die screaming."

"Benny!" scowled Beth.

"Sorry."

"Stacey, I know you're scared," said Mathew putting his arm around her. "I'm scared too, but we don't have much choice. This could be our only chance to put a stop to this. All of it."

"You don't have to come with us. I don't want you to do anything you don't want to do" said Benny. "And that goes for the rest of you. I won't hold it against anyone if they don't want to be part of this crazy suicide plan, cause that's what it will probably be. I still plan to see this through, alone if I have to."

"You won't be alone," said Beth. "I'll be with you."

"I'm not sitting this one out," said Mathew. "You know you can depend on me."

"Me too," said Caroline. "Where Mathew goes, I go too."

"Okay," said Stacey slightly unsure of herself. "Let's do this. I'm in."

"Thanks, Stacey," said Beth as she leaned over and gave her friend a hug. "We can do this. I believe we can."

Stacey smiled nervously back at Beth as she hugged her back with the arm that wasn't holding the shotgun. The commotion of the van driven by Connor down the grassy trail made them break their embrace.

"Okay," he said sticking his head out the window. "This is what I've worked out. Get in, I crash through the gate and we run in. Got it?"

Benny opened the side door and held it open for everyone to jump in.

"Think so," he said as he waited for the others to jump in before getting in himself. He closed the door shut then patted Connor on the shoulder. "If this doesn't go right, I just want to say-"

"Now stop that right now," interrupted Connor. "Don't want to hear any of that soppy crap. We got a world to save, right?"

"Yes, we do," laughed Benny. "Let's go."

Connor drove the van towards the complex wall. As he drove close to it, he managed to attract the attention of the red eyes around it. He continued driving until he reached the far side.

"There's the gate there," he shouted. "Just got to get the bulk of them dicks away from it."

Connor braked hard and stopped the van a stone's throw away. He held the horn down releasing a noisy blast that was heard by every single red eye. They all turned their attention to the van and migrated towards it.

"That's it, you dumb bastards, keep on coming," muttered Connor under his breath.

"This is actually working," said Benny. "Look! They're clearing away from the gate."

The gate was sturdy looking and was newer than the brick wall that surrounded the building which they could see through the bars of the gate. It was a very derelict looking two storey building with boarded up windows. A large garage door, in the line of sight of the gates was now visible and seemed to be the best way in.

Connor put the van in reverse and slowly edged in backwards, the red eyes continuing to be drawn away from the walls and gate.

"Everybody get ready to hang on to something," said Connor as he stopped the van and shifted it into first gear. "You still got the gun, Stacey?"

"Er, yes."

"I think I'm going to need that in a few seconds. Here we go!"
Connor drove the van as fast as he could towards the gate while
swerving around the red eyes. He lowered his head and
clenched his eyes shut as they approached the gate.

"Shit!" he shouted, as the van crashed through, smashing the
windscreen into pieces and causing it to veer to the side while
throwing around everyone inside. He slammed on the brakes
and brought it to a halt as quickly as he could. He wasn't fast
enough to prevent the van crashing through the wooden panel
of the garage door and throwing everyone round a second time.

"Everyone alright? Speak to me, people!" shouted Benny who
found himself lying flat on his back on the van floor. He made
sure he had a hold of the axe then looked around.

"I'm okay," shouted Mathew, pulling out his knife "Caroline?"

"I'm here," she said as she held him tight.

"Oh, Jesus, Jesus, Jesus," shouted a shell shocked Stacey,
trying her to best to compose herself.

"Just breathe, Stacey," reassured Beth, patting her on the back.
"Nice and slow deep breaths."

"As much as it would be nice to take a little breather, I don't
think these fellas are going to give us a break," said Connor as
he opened the driver door and rolled out. "My back's bloody
killing me."

Benny opened the side door of the van and stepped outside.
Connor had managed to drive the van right through the wooden

doors, leaving a huge hole. Already Benny could see the red eyes were fully aware of where the van was and were already coming through the gate.

"We need to move fast," he said holding his hand out and helping the others to get out of the van.

"Here, take this back," said Stacey handing the shotgun back to Connor.

"Thanks, babes," he said, as he took it off her and pointed it to the outside.

"Save it," said Benny, "There's too many of them."

"Aw, you used to be cool," said Connor lowering the gun, and turning around to join the others who were looking around for somewhere to hide.

Which was going to be difficult as there was nowhere to hide. The inside of the building was just a huge empty space of nothingness, like a deserted underground multi storey car park.

"What do we do now?" said Stacey. "There's nowhere to go."

"She's right," said Caroline, looking frantically around. "There's nothing here! Mathew, what do we do?"

Mathew was lost for words. He looked towards Benny.

"Shit! I think we've lost our wheels," said Connor, seeing that the red eyes were now pouring through the hole in the garage door and surrounding the van.

"What do we do now?" cried Caroline.

Connor took aim and fired at the mob of red eyes. Two of them were flung back as chunks of their flesh were shredded off them.

"We better come up with something quick," he shouted, firing a second time and dropping two others in a similar fashion.

"There's a lot of them and these bullets won't last forever."

"Wait," said Beth, catching something out of the corner of her eye. "What's that?"

"What's what?" said Stacey.

Beth ran over to one of the support beams near the far wall. Stacey, Mathew and Caroline followed behind, all unsure on what had caught Beth's attention.

"Benny!" she called out. "Do you still have that card? From that scientist?"

"Yeah, said Benny as he jogged over to her. He pulled it out of his pocket and handed it to her. "What is it?"

A plain metal plate was screwed onto the pillar with a small card sized slot in the middle. Beth pushed the card into the slot, and suddenly a green light appeared all around the edges of the panel

"Just a hunch, which I think had paid off" she said. "This panel looks far too clean and new for my liking."

"You found a way out yet?" shouted over Connor, who had been firing off shots into the crowd of red eyes. A pile of bloodied bodies had built up over the gap which had temporally blocked the way in for the others.

A loud grinding noise was heard from below a section of the floor. They all turned around to see a huge rectangular panel on the floor was tilting downwards.

"Look!" shouted Stacey. "There's a ramp going underground!"

"Where's that lead to?" said Caroline.

"Don't know," said Benny as he walked over to it. "But it's probably our only way out of this."

The lowered panel had formed a ramp descending down below the floor and revealed a large open doorway in the wall that had been hidden.

"Let's go then," said Beth as she took the card out of the slot. She jumped down onto the ramp and led the way towards the entrance. Benny turned around and waved everyone to follow.

"How many shells you got left?" asked Benny to Connor.

"About ten," he said loading two of them into the shotgun. "Including these ones."

"Jesus, I thought you had more than?"

"Yeah, me too. Guess counting isn't my strong point either. Or maybe I got a little carried away."

As Benny and Connor entered the tunnel, a huge metal door came slamming down behind them, startling them both.

"It's alright," said Beth reassuring them as she stepped back from a control panel mounted on the wall. "That was me. I think."

"We can still open that door, right?" said Caroline, looking over at the control panel.

"I think we should leave it shut," said Stacey, gently pulling her away. "Those things are going to be on the other side, trying to get at us."

"So how do we get out? Are we stuck here?" said Caroline starting to panic.

"Come on," said Benny. "Let's see what's down here. And maybe, we can put an end to all this shit."

Chapter 33

The group carried on walking down the faceless white bricked corridor. The ceiling was the height of four men and had fluorescent light tubes all along the roof giving off a blinding white shine.

The further they carried on, the more it became apparent that not only was the corridor slopping down but it was also turning in a clockwise direction.

"It's like a helter skelter," said Beth, as the downward spiral became more pronounced.

"I think it's safe to say we've found the right place," said Connor. "Unless there's another secret underground base totally unrelated to this all that we've accidentally found. Boy, wouldn't that be embarrassing?"

They reached the end of the corridor which opened up into a massive hall. Over at one side was a single army truck. Beth walked over to it to get a closer look.

"Hey, Stacey. Isn't the same type of truck that nearly wiped us out on the road?"

"It looks like it," replied Stacey. "But what does it mean?"

"It means we're definitely in the right place," said Benny. "The trucks, the tape, this base. It all adds up."

"I feel like we're in an episode of Scooby Doo," said Connor as he looked around the very empty hall. "Maybe when we find this one three zero whatever, it will turn out to be an old bitter man in a mask. I woulda gotten away with it if it weren't for you bastard kids."

"Locked," said Mathew as he tried the door to the truck.

"Maybe the back door is open."

"No, it's locked too," shouted Beth from the other side of the truck.

"Where do those doors lead to," said Caroline pointing to two doors in the far corner.

Benny walked over towards them with the others following behind. He looked over towards them before gently pushing slightly each door. Both of them were unlocked.

"Which one should we try first?" he asked.

"We should split up," said Connor. "You and Mathew go through that door and me and the girls will go the other."

They all turned to look at Connor with a look of shock, amazement and disgust.

"I'm joking," he said in a fake flabbergasting voice. "What you think this is? A bloody Scooby Doo cartoon? We'll all stick together and be safe, alright?"

"Can we keep the jokes until this is over?" said Caroline. "My nerves are shot already."

"Fair enough," mumbled Conner, and under his breath added, "it was worth a shot."

Benny pushed the first door open with the axe and walked in. A poorly lit corridor that stretched on for some distance greeted him. Along the left side of the corridor were white wooden doors equally spaced out. Benny crept up to the one closest, turned the handle and pushed it open. He stepped back, holding his axe tight and waited for the door to swing open fully.

Once he was sure there was nothing was going to jump out at him, he peered in. It was dark so he reached around the wall until he found the light switch. He flicked it and the room was lit up. Inside were two army style beds, a table at the side and two chairs. On the other side of the room was a sink with two tooth brushes, toothpaste, soap and razors.

"This corridor must be for dorm rooms," deduced Benny.

"Looks a little basic," said Connor. "At least they kept it clean. They could have made their beds though."

"Now don't tell me you make your bed every morning," said Benny.

"You know what they say, Ben. Cleanliness is next to Godliness, but only in the Irish dictionary."

"Seriously, can we save the jokes until later?" said Stacey. "This place is freaking me out by the second."

"Let's move on then," said Benny. "See what else is down here."

"It's too dark," said Caroline, looking down the poorly lit corridor.

"Must be a light switch or something," said Beth feeling along the walls. "Wait until I get the lights."

"The lights are on already," said Connor walking into the darkness with his shot gun pointed. "They're just broke."

"Connor! Wait!" shouted Beth to no avail.

"Stay here," said Benny to the others as he jogged up behind Connor. "Don't be walking off like this, we need to stick together."

"Jesus, Ben. They can still see me. It's not as if I've disappeared completely."

"I know, it's just..."

Benny stopped dead both in his speech and tracks when they turned into a huge hall on the right side of the corridor.

"Holy donkey balls!" gasped Connor.

Judging from the lay out of the tables and chairs, it was a mess hall and in every sense of the word. Bodies, intact and not so intact and body parts, identifiable and not so identifiable were scattered everywhere. Dried blood that had been splattered all around had left the room covered in a dark brown red motif. The smell wasn't too good either.

"These look like army uniforms," said Connor as he gently kicked over a bloody lump of camouflage cloth and flesh.

"Yeah," replied Benny. "And there's a few white lab coats in here as well. Think this was all talked about on the tape."

A groaning coming from the corner was heard.

"What's that?" said Connor.

"It came from over there," said Benny pointing to an opened door which led to what presumably was the kitchen.

Benny gingerly stepped over the mounds and walked along the bloodied floor towards the kitchen door. Connor followed closely behind him, pointing the shotgun over Benny's shoulder.

Benny peered inside and caught sight of several figures huddled over the floor, seemly picking at something beneath them, and then stuffing it in their mouths. It was a sight that although was now very familiar to them, was still hard to watch. Benny slowly closed the door.

"What? You don't want me to waste them?" whispered Connor.

"No point," said Benny walking back to the corridor. "You're running low on ammo and I don't want to risk getting involved in a melee fight if I can avoid it. We need to get back to the others."

"Yeah, fair enough. Hey, looks like we did split up there, didn't we? Guess we're just as bad as those dicks in the movies."

"You guys find anything?" said Beth as she saw Benny and Connor returning.

"No. Nothing we need worry about," said Benny as he continued to walk towards them. "It's clear here, we need to try the other door."

"Okay, let's do this then," said Mathew, holding his knife up with one hand and holding tight to Caroline with the other. "You guys ready too?"

The girls looked at each other nervously, all knowing that they were getting closer to the end of whatever it was they were on.

"Yes," said Beth confidently. "Let's do this."

"Yeah," said Stacey nervously. "We can do this. We got this far."

"Let's get this over with," said Caroline more annoyed than scared.

"That's the attitude, girls," piped in Connor. "Group hug? No? Well, okay then. Go team!"

Everyone ignored Connor and followed Benny through the door, back into the hall which housed the army trucks.

"Door number two then?" said Benny looking back at everyone.

He pushed it open into another corridor, just like the one they were previously in except it was fully lit and there were rows of doors on either side.

"I'm bloody sick of seeing these corridors," said Connor, as he tried the first door on his right. It was locked. He tried the one opposite and found it locked also. He ran along the corridor trying each one finding them all to be locked.

"Go easy, Connor," shouted Beth.

"I could just blow one of these doors open," said Connor frustrated.

"If you're going to blow any door open, I think you should blow that one," said Benny pointing to the end of the corridor. The corridor opened up at the end into an alcove where a huge set of steel double doors stood. Beside them was another card reader slot on a plane metal sheet mounted on the wall.

"Perhaps you don't need to shoot it, "said Beth as she approached the panel. She took out the card and inserted it into the slot.

"She's good at that," said Connor nudging Stacey. Stacey quickly glanced back in disapproval, while Caroline made her disapproval more apparent.

Like before, blue light lit up from the edges of the panel and then it beeped several times. The doors buzzed and then they both slid back.

Benny was the first through the door. He made sure he remained at the front of the group as he took a good look around the latest room.

It was undoubtedly the main lab that Ryan Purcell had talked about on the tape. The room was almost as large as the first one with the trucks. Along the edge of the room were benches, with computers, microscopes, racks of test tubes and other familiar apparatus that wouldn't look out of place at a school science lab. This wasn't what the group found themselves intrigued by in the slightest. At the front of the room, almost taking centre stage was a large metal cylinder, surrounded by scaffolding and ladders.

"Is that.." started Stacey.

"It must be…" answered Beth.

"What's inside it?" asked Caroline.

Without saying a word Connor walked over towards it and put his head up against the glass.

"I've a very bad feeling we're in a shit load of trouble," he said.

"What is it," said Benny walking towards the cylinder himself. He gently pushed Connor to the side and looked in himself.

"It's empty," said Benny.

"What?" said Beth, who then pushed Benny to the side and looked in herself. "But didn't you say the tape said this there was something kept here."

"Yeah," said Connor. "So where the hell is it?"

Before anyone could answer, a piercing female scream punctured the silence, forcing everyone to perk up and turn behind them. The scream came from Caroline. It didn't take them long to see what see she was screaming at.

Mathew was standing at the back and standing behind him with its claw like hands around his neck was the creature they were looking for.

Chapter 34

It was seven and a half foot tall and was even worse than Ryan's description had portrayed it. It looked like a normal man had been stripped naked, boiled alive then had its skin flailed off and then reattached back to its body inside out. Without any warning, the creature let out an unholy howl as its jaw disconnected like a snake's. In a split second, taking everyone by further surprise it then engulfed Mathew's head entirely in its mouth, and bit down.

Caroline screamed again as the creature yanked its head back up, leaving Mathew's decapitated body turning into a bloody mess as blood spurted up from the hole were his head once was. The creature let go of Mathew's corpse, letting it fall to the bloody pool below it. In a twisted way it appeared to smile over at Caroline while continuing to crunch and chew Mathew's head. She fell to her knees and stared at her boyfriend's body, sobbing uncontrollably.

"I got the bastard!" screamed Connor. He stepped forward, pointed the shotgun towards the creature and fired twice in quick succession. However, just as Connor fired off the first shot, the creature quickly twisted itself down and to the side, avoiding both shots with ease.

"Oh balls!" shouted Connor as he quickly fumbled to get two more shells from his pocket.

Benny charged at the creature, holding the axe above his head and then swung at it when he was in range. In a lightning quick motion the creature grabbed the axe at the middle of the shaft, and pulled it out of Benny's hands.

As it did, the creature yelled out again, but this time it sounded like it was more in pain than a battle cry. Benny looked up and saw the creature holding the axe high while smoke bellowed from its hand. It looked at Benny before throwing the axe down at him.

"Shit," shouted Benny, as he narrowly avoided being hit by his own weapon.

"Benny! Get outta the way!" shouted Connor, who was once again pointing the shotgun at the creature.

Benny dived to the ground as Connor fired off a single shot. As before the creature twisted itself around at a break neck speed and easily avoided the shot. Before Connor could get the second fired the creature moved quickly towards him, taking huge pounding steps. As it passed Caroline, who was still on her knees weeping, it grabbed her by the face, hoisting her up off the ground and held her out as a human shield.

"No!" screamed Beth as she fired continuously at the creature from the side. It took the creature completely by surprise and she was able to fire four shots into its chest before there was only clicking noises when she pulled the trigger. She let go of the gun and let it drop to the floor as she stared at the creature. It looked straight at her, and then looked down at its own chest where the bullets had struck. A black ooze leaked out of the four holes in its skin but from the creature's reaction, it seemed it was more of a slight annoyance than anything else.

It turned its gaze back to Connor who was still desperately trying to get a good shot at the creature without hitting Caroline, whose muffled screams he could still make out. "Bastard! Bastard! Bastard!" he muttered, as he moved around the creature trying his best to get a shot. The creature kept moving as well, then suddenly with a flick of its wrist, Caroline's body jerked forward as the sound of her neck cracking sent a shockwave to everyone's heart.

"It killed her," screamed Connor. "That thing just killed her!" The creature let out a howl as it twisted itself round once more and flung Caroline's body straight at Connor, catching him completely by surprise as it knocked him clean to the floor. The creature turned its gaze towards Beth and once more gave the impression it was giving another one of its twisted smiles. Just as it leaned forward to begin walking towards Beth, it let out a scream of agony.

"Stay away from her!"

Benny had embedded the axe head fully in between where the creatures shoulder blades should have been. The creature shot up straight, and tried desperately to pull out the axe from its back, which was beginning to smoke and sizzle. It stumbled away towards the far end of the lab.

"We have to kill this thing!" said Beth as she ran up to Benny. "What do we have left to fight with?"

"This!"

Benny and Beth both turned around to see Stacey holding Connor's shotgun and aiming towards the creature.

"Get down!" shouted Beth as she pushed Benny to the ground, giving Stacey a clear shot.

Stacey pulled the trigger. The recoil took her so completely by surprise and didn't even yell out when the gun leapt back into her mouth. She let go off it, letting it fall to the ground and held her hands to her mouth. She then looked down to see a small trickle of blood flowing over her fingers. Her eyes widened and she tried her best to refrain from screaming.

On the other side of the lab, her shot had actually managed to do more than Connor was able to do and hit its target in the chest. It screamed out even louder as a large portion of its flesh was blown off with the shot. Black ooze then pumped out from the new hole down the front of its body.

The creature, with great effort reached back and pulled the axe out, taking with it more chunks of its flesh.

"Move!" shouted a barely recovered Connor as he saw the creature swing the axe back. He pulled Stacey out of the way just as the axe spun narrowly past her head.

"That was close," he muttered as he looked back to see the axe disappear behind the scaffolding surrounding the metal cylinder.

"You still got the bullets?" said Benny scrambling over towards him with Beth as he picked up the shotgun and handed it to him.

Before Connor could respond the creature had raced over to him and snatched the shotgun out of his hands.

"Uh, oh," he gasped as the creature snapped it in two right in front of him. It then casually threw the pieces over its shoulder and then made a noise that almost sounded like laughing. Connor looked down at the last handful of shotgun shells he still had left. He looked back up at the creature, which was slowly bringing its face closer to him. He then, in a last ditch desperation attempt, threw the shells at the creatures face. A popping sound was made when each one hit the creature, causing it to ever so slightly flinch. It then looked back at Connor and laughed louder.

"Run for it!" shouted Connor, as he then attempted to kick the creature between the legs, while the rest scrambled. Connor's brave but ultimately foolish move failed, when the creature was able to grab him by the ankle, and then hoist him up like a fisherman displaying his prize catch.

"Oh God!" screamed Beth, as she stopped running once she saw Connor's predicament. "Let him go!"

The creature continued to laugh as it gently swung Connor to and fro, as the girls watched helplessly.

"Better put him down right now," shouted Benny. Everyone turned around to see once again Benny was now brandishing the axe that the creature had tried to throw away. "I know this thing hurts you a lot and if you don't let him go, I'm going to use it to cut your dick off! Lengthwise!"

The creature stopped laughing, held Connor up higher and then looked at him intensively.

"You better let me go, asshole" said Connor trying his best to conceal his nerves. "He's pretty pissed off with what you've done this week."

The creature snorted, and then dropped Connor to the ground. He hit it hard.

"Bastard," muttered Connor, as he struggled to get up to his feet.

Before anyone could breathe a sigh of relief, or think about the next step, the creature quickly reached towards Beth, and grabbed her by the back of the neck. It then hoisted her up in the same manner it did with Connor, and held her out towards Benny to see.

"No!" screamed Benny, who was about to charge at the creature, when it held out its other hand, and waved its finger as if Benny was a naughty child being told to stop.

"Kill it, Benny! Just kill it!" screamed Beth.

Benny looked at Beth dangling then to the creature.

"Please," pleaded Benny, "Let her go."

"You piece of shit," shouted Connor, as Stacey held onto him. "What do you want anyway? Huh?"

The creature snorted once again, then turned to Benny and pointed to the axe.

"You want this? You can have it. Just let her go," said Benny, holding it out to him.

"Benny! No, you can't!" screamed Beth.

The creature grabbed the axe from Benny. It sizzled in its hand for a brief second before it flung it straight up in the air, embedding it into the roof.

"No!" exclaimed Beth in desperation, realising that they had just lost their only weapon that could kill the creature.

"I'm sorry. Beth," he said. "I can't lose you as well as Jason and Pete and Arnold."

Beth closed her eyes as tears flowed down her face.

The creature began to laugh again.

"Why don't you just let Beth go, and come over here and take a big bite out of my head?" shouted Benny. "I don't think you're as bad you think you are."

"Benny, what are you up to?" said Connor quietly to himself.

"You hear me? Come over here, and I'll mess you up big time," shouted Benny with defiance. "I'll kick your ass with my hands behind my back, see?"

"He is up to something," Connor whispered to Stacey.

"Yeah, but what?" she replied.

"I'll even make it easy for you, I'll kneel down for you!" continued Benny. He knelt down on his knees and held his hands behind his back.

"Benny?" said Beth, not sure if perhaps Benny's mind had finally snapped.

"Get ready for something, Stacey" said Connor.

He turned to see Stacey had disappeared from his side and was dashing over to where Mathew's decapitated body lay. He knew something was going to happen, but he didn't know what. All he knew, was he had to get ready for whatever it was.

The creature moved towards Benny and as it walked it let go of Beth, who fell to the ground gentler than Connor did.

"Benny! Run!" she shouted, but was dismayed to see that Benny remained in the same position.

"Beth, you okay?" shouted Stacey as she then dashed over from Mathew's body to her friend.

Benny looked up at the creature who stood right in front of him within grasping distance. It slowly brought its two hands closer to Benny's throat.

Benny then smiled.

"Got you," he said as he quickly jumped up, and then rolled away.

The creature looked down to see his hands were chained together by a pair of pinky fluffy handcuffs. It tried to pull its hands apart and then it let out a terrifying howl when it realised it was burning its wrists.

"You'll find, Mr. Dickface, that those very nice pink cuffs have been sprayed with the same liquid that the axe and bullets were soaked in," said Benny smugly. "You can thank Frankie for that one."

"That's my cue," thought Connor as he ran towards the creature, and dropkicked it to the back of the knee. It lost its balance and fell flat onto its back, nearly landing on Connor who rolled out of the way.

Benny quickly ran over and grabbed the chain of the handcuffs. He held it tight to the ground pinning the creature's arms over its head. Connor jumped onto of the torso of the creature and wrapped his hands around what passed for its throat.

"Get something, something sharp!" shouted Connor, as the creature still thrashed its legs about.

"I've got this," shouted Stacey, holding up the knife that Mathew had previously been using.

"Bring it over now!" yelled Benny, who had placed his knees so they were now on top of the creatures hands.

Stacey and Beth ran over so they were on either side.

"How shall I do this?" asked Stacey holding the knife over the thrashing creature, unsure if she had it in her to kill something, no matter how evil it was.

"We do this together," shouted Beth reaching out and grabbing Stacey's hand that was holding the knife. She pulled it over so the blade was pointed directly over the creature's skull. It looked up and opened his mouth to release a rage filled scream.

"Now!" shouted Benny as he put both his hands on the top of the knife's hilt and pushed down along with the girls as hard as they could. Connor held tightly onto the creature's throat as the knife pierced through the bone between the creature's eyes, and deep into the bloody gory contents inside. Its mouth dropped open as it exhaled for its last time a wail of despair.

"You like that!" yelled Connor, who took his hands off the throat and helped push the knife down further. Black ooze poured out of the entry wound the knife had made as the wail from the creature began to fade. Suddenly there was a breaking noise of the knife exiting through the back of the skull and scratching the floor beneath.

All four of them leaned back and stood up. They looked down at the creature below, looking completely lifeless.

"Is it dead?" said Stacey.

Connor lifted his foot up and brought his heel down on to the hilt of the knife, driving it down further. The face caved in and then was covered with an outpouring of more black ooze from the wound.

"I'd say we done it," said Beth, looking closely at the mess.

"We did," laughed Benny proudly. "Holy shit! We did it! We actually did it!"

"Yeah, I really did it here too," said Connor sheepishly. "I think I've broke my foot."

Chapter 35

After covering up the bodies of Mathew and Caroline and saying a few words, the four of them slowly walked back through the lab and to the ramp that led up towards the outside. Despite the carnage, the loss of life they witnessed and the fatigue they were feeling, they couldn't all but help feel pleased with themselves. However a question remained on their minds. What was waiting for them outside?

As they approached the top of the ramp they could hear voices. Lots of them. The sounds of people shouting and crying but without the anger or violence that they had been so used to over the last few days. It was the sound of confused and lost people. "You hear that?" said Benny excited. "That sounds like people. Real people."

They walked up the ramp, into the car park and past the van which they had used to crash through. Benny ran out to see the red eyes that had previously surrounded the building were all back to normal. They were all confused as to where they were and how they got there, and many of them looked frightened. Some of them were baffled as to why their mouths seemed to have dried blood and what seemed like pieces of raw meat in their mouths.

"Going to be tough explaining that one," mumbled Benny as he watched one young woman picking her teeth and then examining the contents.

"So what should we do now?" said Stacey looking around the best she could as her eyes still adjusted to the light.

"My car's back at the camp," said Beth. "Maybe it's time we went home now. Think the party's over."

"Think you're right," said Connor. "Just go a bit slowly, think I really did my foot there. Looked cool at the time though."

Benny and Beth both laughed as they walked up towards the camp.

"Don't worry, I'll not leave behind, the brave little solider," joked Stacey.

"Thanks," said Connor, nervously. "You know, I was really impressed with you back there,"

"I didn't think I did that much. You guys did more," said Stacey, sheepishly.

"It was a team effort remember." said Connor putting his arm around her and giving her a tight, friendly squeeze. "And the way you took that shotgun and shot that thing, well that really did it for me, girl."

"Really?" said Stacey taken back.

"Yeah, really. To be honest, I didn't think you had it in you. I thought you'd be the sort of girl you'd spend hours and hours on make-up and clothes and have a billion shoes under your bed."

"Well, I wouldn't have that many shoes…"

"Great! You know, you're still a pretty girl. I think that scar will give you a bit of character. Show the world you're not afraid to go there and get down and dirty."

"Scar?"

"Yeah, where the recoil hit you in the face. Well maybe scar's not the right word for it. Maybe an extended beauty dimple or something? I'm sure it'll not be a big deal or anything. It'll probably disappear in a few weeks. You'll still be pretty though, if that helps?"

"Um, thanks?" frowned Stacey, who was truly not sure what to make of what Connor was saying.

"I'm not doing a very good job here, am I?" said Connor sensing it. "How about I just shut up, and you just kiss me like they do in the movies?"

Stacey looked up at Connor, smiled, then leaned in and kissed him.

"Looks like they're getting on well now," said Benny, noticing the kissing couple.

"So they are," said Beth looking over. "You're not jealous, are you?"

"No, not really. Stacey's nice but I don't think of her that way," he said sadly.

Beth nodded and then smiled at him. She stopped walking and grabbed Benny by the hand. She then pulled him towards her so she was facing him.

"Is there someone you really like then? A girl that isn't Stacey, perhaps?" she said with a knowing grin on her face.

Benny looked down towards the ground.

"Benny," she said sternly. "You've saved my life several times this week. There's also a lot of other people who wouldn't be alive if it wasn't for you. Despite losing Jason and your best friend, you've been strong, brave and a leader. We wouldn't have had a chance against whatever the hell that thing was that caused all this shit."

"Yeah," mumbled Benny, still not looking up.

"So why are you still so scared to ask me out," she laughed.

Benny looked up at her, not sure what to say.

"Well?" said Beth, with a cheeky smile on her face.

"Um, Beth, do you want to, I don't know, catch a film or something? Maybe, um, go bowling?"

"I don't think the cinema or the bowling alley is going to be open for quite a while, Benny," she said. "So how about we just skip that bit and go for this."

She leaned towards him and before Benny could reply, she placed her lips on his and kissed him. For a split second Benny was in shock, but then he closed his eyes and reciprocated. He put his arms around her waist and brought her closer to him.

'Seems this weekend wasn't a total disaster in the end,' he thought.

END

Acknowledgements and all that shit...

Much thanks to Darren Saint Darren for creating the incredible cover and promotional material for NABZS. It was a great inspiration during the writing process to get an E-mail from the Saint with some of his early ideas for the cover. Certainly was great motivation to put down my Nintendo DS, leave the rescuing of Princess Zelda to another day and finish the book. If you ever get a chance, do check his other work out on his Facebook page where several bands have commissioned the man to design their album covers, logos and even mascots (he's Ballymena's very own Derrick Riggs).
He has t-shirts and other merchandise which is bloody cool and no doubt if you wore it on a night out, you'd score.

Big thumbs up to Alan 'Uncle Al' Burnside and the other poor tortured souls who had the wonderful pleasure of reading the early drafts. These things unfortunately never come out perfect first time and do take time and time to go over and over and over and over until they're no longer crapish. So thanks again, guys.

A shout out to Team 'Watson Your Face'. Who would have thought running through ten miles of forests, rivers, hills, mud and mountains in Scotland at night during winter in the name of charity could be absolute hell and yet a joy at the same time? So I tip my hat to Neil, Ian, Stephen, Parky, Richard, Adam, Alpha, Fin, Crazy Steve and Emma, Andy and Tim.

And finally but by no means least, the rest of my beautiful and wonderful friends and family, near and far, living and dead (or undead?). If I start to name people, I'll undoubtedly forget to mention someone and I'd end up feeling shit for about ten minutes. So here's my cop out answer. If you've ever had a drink with me, told me an inappropriate joke or had a laugh, gone to a gig or show, discussed what makes a great movie/comic/video game, lent me money, shared a drunken snog, slept on my couch or I've slept on yours, or I don't think you're a tosser...then you know who you are.

And before I finish, I believe there's room in the world of zombies for both walking zombies and running zombies. So let's not fight, eh? As long as they don't glow in daylight, we should be happy.

Suppose I really should mention the wife too. Thanks, Susan.

Printed in Great Britain
by Amazon

19347238R00169